"Look at me, then— are." He indicated with the movement of his hands. "Just one brief eye-to-eye contact, *cara,* and I promise I will step back."

Thinking it was a bit like asking her to strip naked, because making eye contact with Franco had much the same effect on her already edgy senses, Lexi pushed out a short sigh, then lifted up her chin.

He dared to smile, with his lips and his eyes—a tender kind of gentle humor that struck like a flaming arrow directly at her heart. "I wish you weren't so handsome," she told him wistfully. "Why couldn't you have a bigger nose, or something? Or a fat, ugly mouth?"

"You know—" reaching out to run his hands around her slender waist, he carefully drew her closer "—your open honesty will shame the devil one day."

"Are you the devil in question?" She didn't even try to stop her progress toward him.

Franco grimaced. "Probably… I suppose—yes…" he admitted. "Because I am about to break my promise to you and…" He did not bother to finish. He just closed the gap between their mouths.

**All about the author...**
*Michelle Reid*

Reading has been an important part of **MICHELLE REID's** life as far back as she can remember. She was encouraged by her mother, who made the twice-weekly bus trip to the nearest library to keep feeding this particular hunger in all five of her children. In fact, one of Michelle's most abiding memories from those days is coming home from school to find a newly borrowed selection of books stacked on the kitchen table just waiting to be delved into.

There has not been a day since that she hasn't had at least two books lying open somewhere in the house ready to be picked up and continued whenever she has a quiet moment.

Her love of romance fiction has always been strong, though she feels she was quite late in discovering the riches Harlequin Books has to offer. It wasn't long after making this discovery that she made the daring decision to try her hand at writing a Harlequin Presents novel for herself, never expecting it to become such an important part of her life.

**Other titles by Michelle Reid available in eBook:**

Harlequin Presents®

# Michelle Reid

## THE MAN WHO RISKED IT ALL

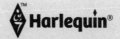

TORONTO NEW YORK LONDON
AMSTERDAM PARIS SYDNEY HAMBURG
STOCKHOLM ATHENS TOKYO MILAN MADRID
PRAGUE WARSAW BUDAPEST AUCKLAND

Recycling programs
for this product may
not exist in your area.

ISBN-13: 978-0-373-13060-3

THE MAN WHO RISKED IT ALL

Copyright © 2012 by Michelle Reid

www.Harlequin.com

**Printed in U.S.A.**

# THE MAN WHO
# RISKED IT ALL

# PROLOGUE

A FEVER of hopeful expectancy had spread through the crowds waiting to see if the race would begin. Suited up and ready to go, Franco Tolle stood inside the *White Streak* team marquee with his safety helmet held in the crook of his arm and his eyes fixed on the monitor, watching for the race organisers' decision to show up on the screen. The wind had picked up, whipping the glass-smooth surface of the Mediterranean into a turbulent boil—not ideal conditions in which to race notoriously temperamental powerboats at sixty metres per second.

'What do you think?' Marco Clemente, his co-driver, came up beside him.

Franco offered a shrug in response. The truth was he wasn't worried so much by the racing conditions as he was by Marco's determination to race with him today.

'Are you sure you are up for this?' he questioned, keeping his voice level and his eyes fixed on the monitor screen.

Marco hissed out an impatient breath. 'If you don't want me in the boat with you, Franco, then just damn well say so.'

And there was the reason why Franco had asked the question in the first place. Marco was on edge, uptight, volatile. He'd spent the last hour pacing the marquee, snapping at anyone who spoke to him, and now he was snapping at Franco. It was not the best frame of mind for him to be in control of the boat's powerful throttle.

'In case you have forgotten, Franco, half of *White Streak* belongs to me—even if you are the one with the design and build genius.'

The petulance in his tone made Franco set his teeth together to stop him saying something he might regret. So they co-owned *White Streak*. So they'd raced both her and her sister boat across Europe under the co-owned White Streak company name for the last five years. But this would be the first time in three of those years that they would be climbing into the same boat together. This was the first time that Franco had given into the pressure and agreed to let Marco take the seat next to him.

And why had he done that? Because the championship hung in the balance with this one last race of the season and his usual co-driver had gone down with the flu yesterday. Marco was, without question, the best man to have sitting in Angelo's place when the stakes were this high, so he'd convinced himself that despite the rift in their friendship the two of them could be professional about this. What he had not known until he'd turned up here today was that Marco was not behaving like the laid-back guy everyone was used to seeing around the place.

'We used to be good friends,' Marco husked with low-voiced intensity. 'For almost all our lives we were the closest of friends. Then I made one small mistake and you—'

'Sleeping with my wife was not a small mistake.'

As if the wind outside had found its way into the tent, the chill of Franco's voice struck through his own protective clothing to his skin.

Marco seemed to breathe that chill in deep. 'Lexi was not your wife back then.'

'No.' Franco turned his head to look at Marco for the first time since the conversation had begun. They stood the same height, shared the same lean athletic build, the same age and the same nationality—but there the similarities ended. For where Marco was fair-haired, with blue eyes, Franco was dark: dark hair, dark eyes, a darker demeanour altogether. 'You, however, were my closest friend.'

Marco tried to hold his gaze. Remorse and frustration vied inside him for a couple of seconds before he sighed and looked away.

'What if I told you it never happened?' he posed abruptly. 'What if I said I made up the whole thing to break the two of you up?'

'Why would you want to?'

'Why would you want to throw your life away on a teenager?' Marco hit back, and revealed that frustration had won out over remorse. 'You still married her anyway, and left me feeling like the worse bastard alive. And Lexi did not even know I'd said anything to you, did she? You didn't tell her.'

As grim and silent as a corpse, Franco looked back at the monitor screen, the naturally sensual shape to his mouth clamping into a hard straight line.

'She can't have known,' Marco muttered, as if he was talking to himself. 'She was too nice to me.'

'Is there a purpose in this conversation?' Franco asked with a sudden flash of irritation. 'We have a race to attend to, and it must be obvious that I have no wish to discuss the past with you.'

'OK, *signori*, we have the go!' As if on cue, the shout from their team manager across the tent broke through the tension eddying around the two men.

Franco began to walk away, but Marco grabbed his arm to hold him still.

'For God's sake, Franco,' he murmured urgently. 'I'm sorry if I messed things up between you and Lexi, but she has been out of your life for over three years now! Can't we put the whole stupid incident behind us and go back to how we—?'

'Shall I tell you why you've decided to drag all of this up?' Franco swung back to him, icy contempt contorting his face now. 'You are in debt to White Streak to the tune of millions. You are scared because you know you need my goodwill to keep that ugly truth under wraps. You have heard the rumours that I am thinking of pulling the plug on powerboat racing and it is scaring you to death—because you know the whole financial mess you've placed us in is likely to blow up in your face. And just for the record,' he concluded icily, 'your lousy attempt at an apology for what you did has come three and a half years too damn late.'

Tugging his arm free, Franco turned away from Marco's frozen expression. In truth, he hadn't expected Marco to drag this up—and it didn't help the way he was feeling to know that back in his apartment divorce papers from Lexi sat waiting for him to find the stomach to read them.

He strode out of the marquee into the hot sunlight, cold anger fizzing like iced nitrogen in his blood. This was Livorno; his home crowd was out there. But he barely heard their rousing cheer. A red mist had risen across his eyes, in the centre of that his once closest friend lay entwined in the heaving throes of passion with the only woman he had ever loved. He had lived with that image ever since Marco had planted it in his head almost four years ago. He had taken it with him into his brief marriage to Lexi. It had coloured the way he had treated her and even made him suspect that the child she had carried was not his. It had changed the pattern of his life. It had embittered him until there was nothing left of the man he'd used to be, and when Lexi had miscarried the baby that image had shadowed the way he had reacted to the loss.

And the hell of it was that Marco was right: Lexi had never known why he'd behaved that way. The one small salve to his own wounded pride was that she'd never known how her betrayal of him with his best friend had broken his damn stupid, gullible heart.

Like a nemesis he could not shake off, Marco appeared at his shoulder again. 'Franco, *amico*, I need you to listen—'

'Don't speak to me about the past,' Franco cut in harshly, before Marco could say any more. 'Focus instead on the job in hand, or I will take the decision to fold up the White Streak company. And the financial mess you've placed it in will come out.'

'But you will ruin me,' Marco breathed hoarsely. 'My family's reputation will be—'

'Precisely.'

He watched Marco go pale, aware of the reason behind his terror. The famous Clemente name was synonymous with fine wines, honesty and charity. It headed some of the biggest charitable organisations in Italy alongside the Tolle name. Their two families had been close for as far back as he could remember—which was the reason he'd kept his rift with Marco so low-key. They still shared a business relationship. They met often at charitable and social events. He'd allowed Marco to laugh off rumours about the cooling of their friendship, and he knew he'd let him get away with it because it was less cutting to his ego than to let anyone learn the real truth.

'Hey you guys, wave to the crowd,' their team manager prompted from behind them.

Like an obedient puppet Franco raised his arm and waved while beside him Marco did the same thing, switching on his famously brilliant smile and charming everyone as he always did. Franco put on his helmet to give his hands something else to do. The moment he did so he lost his own smile. The two of them climbed into the boat's open cockpit. They strapped themselves in. Their race advisor was droning the usual information into his earpiece about wind speeds, the predicted height and length of the ocean swell. They did their pre-start checks, working with the unison of two people used to knowing what the other was thinking all the time. They had been childhood friends, through adolescence and into adulthood together. He would have staked his life on Marco always being there as a deeply loyal friend through to his dotage. Growing old together, kids, grandkids… Warm summer evenings spent watching the sun go down while drinking the best wine the Clemente cellars had to offer and reminiscing about the good old times.

The twin engines fired, their throaty roar a sweet song to Franco's marine engineer's ears. They took her out towards the start line—a streak of bright white amongst the dozen other powerboats splashing the glistening ocean with bright primary colours and bold sponsor logos, all of them holding back on the throttle like crouching dragons, ready to roar into action the split second they were given the go.

He glanced sideways at Marco. Franco didn't know why he did it—the old sixth sense they'd used to share making him do it. Marco had turned his head and was looking at him. There was something written in his eyes…a stark desperation that clutched like a giant fist at Franco's chest.

Marco broke the contact by turning away again, then Franco heard the low sound of Marco's voice in his ear. *'Sono spiacente, il mio amico.'*

Franco was still fighting to grasp what Marco had said to him as the engines gave a throaty roar and they shot forward. It took all of Franco's concentration to keep them on a straight line.

*Too fast*, his brain was registering starkly. Marco had just said he was sorry, and he was taking them out much too fast…

# CHAPTER ONE

LEXI was in a meeting when the door to Bruce's office suddenly flew open and Suzy, the very new junior assistant, burst in.

'Sorry to interrupt,' she rushed out breathlessly, 'but Lexi has just got to see this—'

Her riot of blonde curls bouncing around a pretty face flushed with excitement, Suzy snatched up the television remote from where it lay next to the coffee machine and aimed it at the television. Everyone else gaped at her, wondering where she'd got the nerve to barge in here like this.

'A friend sent this news link to my Twitter,' she explained, hurriedly flicking through channels. 'I'm seriously not into mega crashes, so I almost stopped watching, but then your face flashed up on the screen, Lexi, and they mentioned your name!'

Crystal blue waters topped by deep azure skies suddenly filled the fifty-inch flat screen. A second later half a dozen long streaks of raw engine power suddenly shot across the water, flying like majestic arrows and kicking up huge plumes of foaming white spray in their wake. Before anyone else had even clicked on what was happening, an icy chill of recognition made Lexi jerk to her feet.

High-speed powerboat racing was for the super-rich and reckless only—the whole sleek, surging, testosterone-packed spectacle was a breathtaking display of excess. Excess money, excess power, excess ego—and an excessive flouting of the risks and the dangers that held most people awestruck. But for Lexi it was like watching her worst nightmare play out in front of her eyes, for she knew what was about to happen next.

'No,' she whispered tautly. 'Please switch it off.'

But no one was listening to her, and, anyway, it was already too late. Even as she spoke the nose of the leading craft hit turbulence and began to lift into the air. For a few broken heartbeats the glistening white craft stood on its end and hovered like a beautiful white swan rising up from sea.

'Keep watching.' Suzy was almost dancing on the spot in anticipation.

Lexi grabbed hold of the edge of the table as the mighty powerboat performed the most shockingly graceful pirouette, then began flipping over and over, as if it was performing some wildly exciting acrobatic trick.

But this was no trick, and two very human bodies were visible inside the boat's open cockpit. Two reckless males, revelling in sleek supercharged power that had now turned into a violent death trap as shards of debris were hurled out in all directions, spinning like lethal weapons through the air.

'This highly dangerous sport suffers at least one fatality each season,' some faceless narrator informed them. 'Due to choppy conditions off the coast of Livorno there had been disputes as to whether this race should begin. The leading boat had reached top speed when it hit turbulence. Francesco Tolle can be seen being thrown clear.'

'Oh, my God, that's a body!' somebody gasped out in horror.

'His co-driver Marco Clemente remained trapped underwater for several minutes before divers were able to release him. Both men have been airlifted to hospital. As yet unconfirmed reports say that one man is dead and the other is in a grave condition.'

'Catch her, someone.' Lexi heard Bruce's sharp command as her legs gave way beneath her.

'Here…' Someone leapt up and took hold of her arm to guide her back down onto her chair.

'Put her head between her knees,' another voice advised, while someone else—Bruce again—ground out curses at Suzy for being such a stupid, insensitive idiot.

Lexi felt her head being thrust downwards but she knew even as she let them manhandle her that it wasn't going to help. So she just sat there, slumped forward, with her hair streaming down in front of her like a rippling river of burnished copper, and listened to the newsreader map out Francesco's twenty-eight years as if he was reading out his obituary.

'Born into one of Italy's wealthiest families, the only son of ship-building giant Salvatore Tolle, Francesco Tolle left his playboy ways behind him after his brief marriage to child star Lexi Hamilton broke down…'

The ripple of murmurs in the room made Lexi shiver, because she knew a photograph of her with Franco must have flashed up on the screen. Young—he would look young, and carelessly happy, because that was how—

'Tolle concentrates his energies on the family business these days, though he continues to race for the White Streak powerboat team—a company he set up five years ago with his co-driver Marco Clemente, from one of Italy's major wine-making families. The two men are lifelong friends, who…'

'Lexi, try and drink some of this.'

Bruce gently pushed her hair back from her face so he could press a glass of water to her lips. She wanted to tell him to leave her alone so she could just listen, but her lips felt too numb to move. Locked in a fight between herself, Bruce and the sickening horror she had just witnessed, suddenly she saw Franco.

*Her* Franco, dressed in low riding cut-offs and a white T-shirt that moulded to every toned muscle in his long, bronzed frame. He was standing at the controls of a slightly less insane kind of speedboat, his darkly attractive face turned towards her and laughing, because he was scaring the life out of her as he skimmed them across the water at breakneck speed.

'Don't be such a wimp, Lexi. Come over here to me and just feel the power...'

'I'm going to be sick,' Lexi whispered.

Squatting down in front of her, the oh-so-elegant and super-cool Bruce Dayton almost tumbled onto his backside in an effort to get out of the way of the threat. Stumbling to her feet, Lexi stepped around him and moved like a drunk across the room, a trembling hand clamped across her mouth. Someone opened the door for her and she staggered through it, making it into the cloakroom only just in time.

Franco was dead. Her dizzy head kept on chanting it over and over. His beautiful body all battered and broken, his insatiable lust for danger brutally snuffed out.

'No...' she groaned, closing her eyes and slumping back against the cold tiled wall of the toilet cubicle.

'Not I, *bella mia*. I am invincible...'

Almost choking on a startled gasp—because she felt as if Franco had whispered those words directly into her ear— Lexi opened her eyes, their rich blue-green depths turned black with shock. He was not there, of course. She was alone in her white-walled prison of agony.

Invincible.

A strangled laugh broke free from her throat. No one was invincible! Hadn't he already proved that to himself once before?

A tentative knock sounded on the cubicle door. 'You OK, Lexi?'

It was Suzy, sounding anxious. Making an effort to pull herself together, Lexi ran icy cold trembling fingers down the sides of her turquoise skirt. Turquoise like the ocean, she thought hazily. Franco liked her to wear turquoise. He said it did unforgivably sexy things to her eyes...

'Lexi...?' Suzy knocked on the cubicle door again.

'Y-yes,' she managed to push out. 'I'm all right.'

But she wasn't all right. She was never going to be all right again. For the last three and a half years she had fought to keep Franco pushed into the darkest place inside her head, but now a door had opened and he was right here, confronting her when it was too late for her to—

Oh, dear God, what are you thinking? You don't know he's dead! It might be Marco—

It might be Marco.

Was that any better?

*Yes*, a weak, cruel, wicked voice inside her head whispered, and she hated herself for letting it.

Suzy was waiting for her when Lexi stepped out of the toilet cubicle, her pretty face clouded by discomfort and guilt. 'I'm so sorry, Lexi,' she burst out. 'I just saw your face and—'

'It doesn't matter,' Lexi cut in quickly, because the other girl looked so upset and young.

The same age Lexi had been when she'd first met Franco, she realised. Why was it that, at only twenty-three now, she suddenly felt so old?

'Bruce is threatening to sack me,' Suzy groaned, while Lexi stood at a basin washing her hands without being aware that she was doing it. 'He said he doesn't need a stupid person working here because we have enough of those, what with the wannabe starlets we...'

Lexi stopped listening. She was staring in the mirror at

the small triangle of her face framed by her rippling mane of copper-brown hair.

'It catches fire in the sunset,' Franco had whispered once as he ran his long fingers through its silken length. 'Hair the colour of finely spun toffee, skin like whipped cream, and lips…mmm…lips like delicious crushed strawberries.'

'That's so corny, Francesco Tolle. I thought you had more style that that.'

'I do where it counts, *bella mia*. See—I will show you…'

No crushed strawberries colouring her lips now, Lexi noticed. They looked colourless and faded.

'And you haven't been with him for years, so it never entered my head that you might still care about him.'

Lexi watched her eyelids fold down over her eyes then lift up again. 'He's a human being, Suzy, not an inanimate object.'

'Yes…' The younger girl sounded guilty again. 'Oh, but he's so gorgeous, Lexi.' She sighed dreamily. 'All that dark, brooding sexiness… He could be one of the actors we have on our…'

Lexi tuned the younger girl out again. She knew Suzy had no idea what she was talking about. She didn't mean to hurt, prattling on like that; she was just doing a really bad job of making amends for the huge gaffe she had made, but—

She turned and walked out of the cloakroom, leaving Suzy chatting to an empty space. Her legs felt weak and seriously unwilling to do what she wanted them to do. After she'd shut herself into her own office she just stood there, staring out at nothing. She felt hollow inside from the neck down, except for the tight little fizz of sensation currently clustering around the walls of her heart, which she knew was slowly eating away at her self-control.

'Lexi…'

The door behind her had opened without her hearing it. She turned that unblinking stare on Bruce, lean and sleek, very good-looking in a fair-skinned and sharp-featured kind of way. The grim expression on his face sent a wave of knee-knocking alarm shunting down through her whole frame.

'Wh—What?' she jerked out, knowing that something else truly devastating was about to come at her.

Stepping fully into the room, Bruce closed the door, then came to take hold of her arm. Without saying a word he led her to the nearest chair. As she sank down into it Lexi felt tears start to sting the backs of her eyelids and her mouth wobbled.

'You…you'd better tell me before I have hysterics,' she warned unsteadily.

Leaning back against her desk, Bruce folded his arms. 'There is a telephone call for you. It's Salvatore Tolle.'

Franco's father? Twisting her fingers together on her lap, Lexi closed her eyes again—tight. There was only one reason she could think of that would force Salvatore Tolle to speak to her. Salvatore hated her. He claimed she had ruined his son's life.

'A cunning little starlet willing to prostitute her body to you for the pot of gold.'

She'd overheard Salvatore slicing those cutting words at Franco. She did not know what Franco had said in response because she'd fled in a flood of wild, wretched tears.

'I asked him to hold,' said the indomitable Bruce, who bowed to no one—not even a heavyweight like Salvatore Tolle. 'I thought you could do with a few minutes to…to get your act together before you listened to what he has to say.'

'Thanks,' she mumbled, opening her eyes to stare down at her tensely twined fingers. 'Did…did he tell you wh—why he was calling?'

'He wouldn't open up to me.'

Attempting to moisten the inside of her dry mouth, Lexi nodded, then made an effort to pull herself together yet again.

'OK.' She managed to stand up somehow. 'I had better talk to him then.'

'Do you want me to stay?'

Well, did she? The truth was she didn't have an answer to that question. In her life to date, first as a fifteen-year-old thrust into fame by the starring role she'd taken in a low-budget movie that had surprised everyone by taking the world by storm, Bruce had already played a big part—working alongside her actress mother, Grace, as her agent. Later, when Lexi had gone off the rails and walked away from her shining career to be with her handsome Italian boyfriend, Bruce had not allowed her to lose touch with him. When her mother had died suddenly, Bruce had been ready to offer her his support. But back then she'd still had Franco. Or she'd believed she still had Franco. It had taken months of pain and heartache before she'd finally given in and flown home to Bruce in a storm of heartbreak and tears.

Now she worked for him at his theatrical agency. The two of them worked well together: she understood the minds of his temperamental clients and he had years of rock solid theatrical experience. Somewhere along the way they had become very close.

'I'd better do this on my own.' Lexi made the decision with the knowledge that this was something Bruce could not fix for her.

He remained silent for a moment, his expression revealing not a single thing. Then he gave a nod of his head and straightened up from the desk. Lexi knew she'd hurt his feelings, knew he must feel shut out; but he'd also understand why she had refused his offer to stay. For the phone call involved Franco, and where he was concerned not even Bruce was going to be able to catch her when she fell apart if the news was bad. So she preferred to fall apart on her own.

'Line three,' was all he said, indicating the phone on her desk before he strode back across her office.

Lexi waited until the door shut behind him and then turned to stare down at the phone for a few seconds, before tugging in a breath and reaching out with a trembling hand.

'*Buongiorno, signor,*' she murmured unsteadily.

Across hundreds of miles of fibre-optic line a pause developed that made her heart pump that bit more heavily and her fingers clench around the telephone receiver so tightly they hurt. Then the emotionally thickened voice of Salvatore Tolle sounded in her ear.

'It is not a good day, Alexia,' he countered heavily. 'Indeed, it is a very bad day. I assume you have heard the news about Francesco?'

Lexi closed her eyes as a wave of dizziness broke over her. 'Yes,' she breathed.

'Then I can keep this conversation brief. I have made arrangements for you to travel to Livorno. A car will collect you from your apartment in an hour. My plane will fly you to Pisa and someone will collect you from there. When you reach the hospital you will need to show proof of who you are before you will be allowed to see my son, so make sure you have the relevant—'

'Francesco is—alive?' she shrilled on a thick intake of air, feeling as if someone had hit her hard in the solar plexus.

Another pause on the line pounded and thumped in Lexi's head for a couple of seconds before she heard a softly uttered curse.

'You believed he was dead. My apologies,' Franco's father offered brusquely. 'In the concern and confusion since the accident it had not occurred to me that reports have been confused about... *Si.*' His voice sank low and thickened again as he gave her the confirmation she was waiting so desperately to hear. 'Francesco is alive. I must warn you, however, that he has sustained some serious injuries. Though how the hell he...'

He stopped again, and Lexi could feel the fight he was having with his emotions. Trapped in a spinning swirl of aching relief and fresh alarm due to those injuries he'd mentioned, she recognised that Franco's father must be suffering from a huge shock himself. Francesco was his only child. His adored, his precious, thoroughly spoiled son and heir.

'I'm—sorry you've been put through this,' she managed to whisper.

'I don't need your sympathy.' His voice hardening, Salvatore fired the words at her like a whip.

If she'd had it in her Lexi would have smiled, for she could understand why this man did not want sympathy from her. Loathing the likes of which Salvatore felt for her did not fade away with the passage of time.

'I simply expect you to do what must be done,' he continued more calmly. 'You are needed here. My son is asking for you, therefore you will come to him.'

Go—to Franco? For the first time since the news had tossed her into a dark pit of shock, Lexi blinked and saw daylight. It was one thing to know that Franco had finally taken one wild risk too many, and even to stand here experiencing the full horror of the result, but—go to him?

'I'm sorry, I can't do that.' It felt as if the words had peeled themselves off the walls of her throat, they were so difficult to utter.

'What do you mean, you cannot?' Salvatore ground out. 'You are his wife. It is your duty to come here!'

His wife. How very odd that sounded, Lexi thought as she twisted around to face the window, her eyes taking on a bleak blue glint. Her duty to Franco as his wife had ended three and a half years ago, when he—

'His estranged wife,' she corrected. 'I'm sorry that Francesco has been injured, *signor*. But I am no longer a part of his life.'

'Where is your charity, woman?' her father-in-law hissed in an icy tone that was more in keeping with the man Lexi remembered. 'He is bleeding and broken! He has just lost his closest friend!'

'M-Marco is…dead?' It was yet another shock that held Lexi frozen as the shattering chill of loss seemed to crystallise her flesh.

She stared blindly at the grey skies beyond her office window and saw the handsome laughing face of Marco Clemente. Her heart squeezed with aching grief and the sheer unfairness of it. Marco had never done a bad thing to anyone. He'd been the easygoing one of the two lifelong friends. Where Franco had always been the high charged extrovert, the reckless daredevil, Marco had tagged along because, he'd once told her, he was lazy. It was easier to go with Franco's flow than waste energy trying to swim against it.

Knowing Franco as she did, he was probably crucifying himself right now for involving Marco in his thirst for danger and speed. He would be blaming himself for Marco's death.

'I'm so very sorry,' she whispered across the fresh ache in her throat.

'Si,' Salvatore Tolle acknowledged. 'It is good to know that you feel sadness for Marco. Now I ask you again—will you come to my son?'

'Yes.' Lexi said it without thought or hesitation this time, for no matter how hurt and bitter she felt about Franco, his losing Marco had just changed everything.

Marco and Franco… One without the other was like day without night.

Lowering the phone back onto its rest, Lexi began to shiver again. She just could not stop herself. Lifting a hand to her eyes, she covered the threat of tears stinging there and wished she knew if she was feeling like this because she was relieved that Franco was alive or because poor Marco was…not.

'He's alive, then?'

Spinning around to find that once again Bruce had entered

the room without her hearing him, Lexi pressed her quivering lips together and nodded her head.

Bruce's slender lips twisted into a grimace. 'I thought the lucky swine would be.'

'There is no luck involved in being flung through the air with a load of lethal debris, Bruce!' Lexi reacted fiercely.

'And the other one—Marco Clemente?'

Wrapping her arms tightly around her body, she gestured a mute negative.

'Poor devil,' he murmured.

At least that comment conveyed no sarcasm, she noticed. She pulled in a deep, fortifying breath of air. 'I am going to have to take some time off.'

Bruce stood regarding her through narrowed eyes and Lexi could tell that he was not impressed by that announcement. 'So the Tolle effect still holds strong with you, then?' he said eventually. 'You're going to go to him.'

'It would be wrong of me not to.'

'Even though you are in the process of divorcing him?'

Flushing in response to that challenging question, Lexi half wished that she had not told Bruce that the papers had gone out to Francesco's lawyers two weeks ago.

'That isn't relevant in this situation,' she defended. 'Marco and Franco were like twin brothers. It's only right and fitting that we put our differences aside at a time of tragedy like this.'

'That's just bull, Lexi,' Bruce denounced. 'I'm the guy you ran to when your lousy marriage blew up in your face,' he reminded her with sardonic bite. 'I saw what he did to you. I mopped up the tears. So if you think I am going to stand by in silence and watch you walk back into that poisonous relationship then you can just think again.'

Raising her chin, she turned back to face him. 'I'm not about to walk into a relationship with Franco.'

'Then what *are* you doing?'

'Visiting a grieving and seriously injured man!'

'For what purpose?'

Opening her lips to let fly with a heated answer, Lexi flailed for a second and closed her lips again.

'You still love him,' Bruce stated contemptuously.

'I don't love him.' Walking around her desk, she found herself making hard work of hunting through drawers for her bag.

'You still lust after him, then.'

'I do not!' She found the bag and pulled it out of the drawer.

'Then why are you going?' Bruce persisted doggedly as he prowled towards her, reminding her of a sleek hunting dog gnawing on a particularly tough bone.

'I'm only taking a couple of days off, for goodness' sake!' Lexi breathed out heavily.

'Did he find time to come to *your* bedside when you were losing his baby?' Bruce thrust the words at her like a fisted punch. 'No. Did he give a damn that you were heartbroken, frightened and alone? No,' he punched again. 'He was too busy rolling around in a bed somewhere with his latest bit of skirt. It took him twenty-four hours to turn up, and by then the well-laid bitch had made sure you knew where he'd been. You owe him nothing, Lexi!'

'None of that means that I have to behave as badly as he did!' Lexi cried out, pale as parchment now, because everything he had just said was so painfully true. 'He's hurt, Bruce, and I liked Marco. Please try to understand that I would not be able to live with myself if I didn't go!'

'At the expense of us?'

The *us* held Lexi trapped as she stared at the sharply attractive man standing in front of her desk, looking the epitome of sartorial elegance in a cool grey suit, and she felt the ache of wretched tears return to her throat. Bruce was thirty-five years old to her twenty-three, and the glossy patina of his maturity and sophistication sometimes threatened to drown her in intimidating waves. The cold anger glinting in his pale blue eyes, the cynical edge to his grimly held mouth…Bruce rarely showed this side of himself to her, and in truth she'd never dreamed he would do this—bring out into the open what the two of them had been carefully skirting around for months. Bruce was her mentor, her saviour, her closest friend, and she loved him so much—in a very special way she reserved just for him.

But not in the way she knew he wanted her to love him, though she so desperately wished that she could.

'No, forget I said that.' He sighed suddenly, throwing out a hand as if he was tossing the explosive challenge aside. 'I'm angry because the—' He stopped to utter a softly bitten curse before he continued, 'Franco has raised his handsome head again just at the point when you were…' A short sigh censored the next words too. 'Go,' he sanctioned in the end, turning away to stride back to the door. 'Perhaps seeing him again after this length of time will make you recognise that you've grown up, while he's still the… I just hope you find closure on your feelings for him and when you get back you will finally be able to get on with the rest of your life without that bastard in it!'

Standing behind her desk, clutching her bag to her front and fighting the urge to run after him and beg him to understand, Lexi knew right then, in that struggling moment, that something else had just been brought to a close: her long relationship with Bruce. Tears burned hot as she took on board what that revelation truly meant. She'd been a fool—unfair, selfish. She'd known how he felt about her but had crushed the knowledge down so she didn't have to face up to it and deal with it. In the last few months she'd even started to convince herself that an intimate relationship between them would be possible—they worked so well together and liked each other so much.

But liking wasn't enough, and she knew it—had probably always known it. She had not been playing fair with Bruce from the moment she'd recognised how his feelings towards her had changed from good friend and mentor to prospective lover.

With her tongue cleaving tautly to the roof of her mouth and her lips pinned tightly together in an effort to stop them from trembling, Lexi dragged on her coat. She didn't have the time right now, but when she got back from Italy she knew that she and Bruce were going to have to have a long talk about where their relationship was heading.

Or not heading, she amended bleakly. If today's shock had done anything, it had made her take a hard look at herself. She was only twenty-three years old, and already she'd fallen in love with a rich, irresponsible playboy, become pregnant with his child, become his wife, learned how to hate him for using her, learned how much he'd resented her for turning him into a husband, lost their baby and lost him.

*So why are you walking back into his life?*

Lexi was still grappling with that question late that afternoon as she made her way out onto Pisa's busy airport concourse, a long delicately built figure of medium height, wearing skinny stretch blue jeans and a soft grey jacket, with a scarf looped loosely around her throat. Her hair was loose, floating around her strained, pale face; and her tense blue-green eyes were scanning the crowds in front of her for a sign to tell her who would be there to pick her up. Almost immediately she spotted a familiar face.

Pietro, a short, dapper man with a shock of silver hair and smooth olive skin stood waiting for her by the barrier. Pietro was Salvatore's personal chauffeur, and his wife Zeta was housekeeper at the fabulous Castello Monfalcone, the Tolle private estate situated just outside their home town of Livorno. Both Pietro and Zeta had always been coolly polite to Lexi; that had been a small something in a place filled with animosity and resentment.

Striding forward, Pietro greeted her sombrely. 'It is good to see you again, *signora*, though not so good the circumstances.'

'No,' Lexi agreed.

Taking charge of her small bag, he indicated that she follow him. Ten minutes later he was driving her towards Livorno in the kind of luxury car she had once turned her back on without a single pang of regret. Strange, really, she pondered as she stared out at the familiar sights sliding by the car window. She had come to love Livorno itself during her brief stay there, even if she'd hated everything else.

Her escape, she recalled, from tension and disapproval. A nineteen-year-old pregnant married woman—still just a girl, really—made to feel like an interloper and an outcast at the same time. Salvatore hadn't been able to stand looking at her. Francesco had reminded her of a beautiful golden eagle who'd had his fabulous wings clipped and his freedom to fly wherever he wanted to ripped away. He'd snapped at anyone who dared to approach him, picked fights—with his father most of all. He'd resented Salvatore's attitude towards Lexi, to his marriage, to their coming child. He'd hated it that he couldn't defend her because he had never been certain that she hadn't set him up in a baby trap as his father had accused her of doing.

'Why did you bother to marry me?'

Lexi moved with a jolt as her own shrill voice echoed inside her head.

'What else was I supposed to do with you? Leave you and the baby to starve on the streets?'

*When true love turns bad,* Lexi thought bleakly. She was still able to recall the aching throb of raw hurt she'd carried around with her for long lonely months until…

Oh, bring on the violins, Lexi, she told herself impatiently. So you had this amazing love affair with this amazingly sexy and gorgeous playboy and you got yourself pregnant? So you married the playboy and lived to regret it and lost your baby—which, to most people, was a huge relief? Grieve for your baby, but don't grieve for a marriage that should never have happened in the first place. And *don't*, she warned herself sternly, go all self-pitying again, because it earned you nothing back then and will earn you even less now.

The car slowed down and she focused back on her surroundings as they turned in through the hospital gates. It was a bright white, very modern, very exclusive place, set in the seclusion of its own private grounds.

It was the same hospital she had been rushed to three and a half years ago. As she climbed out of the car and looked at the building a whole rush of old emotions erupted inside. She did not want to walk back in there. She felt herself go cold at the thought. Her baby… her tiny baby…had been stillborn within those walls, those whisper-quiet corridors, that luxury accommodation.

'Signor Salvatore asked me to accompany you, *signora*.' Pietro's arrival at her side made Lexi jump. She blinked, fighting—*fighting*—to push back the memories, the strangling agony of old feelings, of painful emptiness and grief.

'It is this way…'

Somehow she placed one foot in front of the other. A security man guarding the front doors asked to see her passport before he would allow her to step inside. Her lips and her mouth felt paper dry as she rummaged in her bag to find it while Pietro became angrily animated, insisting that the precaution was not necessary when he could vouch for *la signora's* authenticity.

Lexi just wished he would leave the guard to do his job. This was all beginning to be too much for her. Francesco didn't need her. It wasn't as if he was alone in the world. He had a huge network of family and friends who had to be more than willing to gather around him. If she had an ounce of good sense she would turn around and walk right back out of there.

But she didn't turn and walk away. She followed Pietro across the hospital lobby and into a waiting lift that carried them up. Yet another walk down a hushed white corridor and Pietro was opening a door and standing back to allow Lexi to precede him inside. Beginning to feel as if she was floating on a current of icy air now, Lexi filled up her lungs and stepped into the room.

It took a couple of foggy seconds for her to realise that this was an anteroom. Comfortable chairs stood grouped around a low table topped by a small stack of thick glossy magazines. The aroma of fresh coffee permeated the air. A pretty nurse with her ebony hair neatly contained beneath a white cap sat at a desk behind a computer monitor.

She looked up at Lexi and smiled, 'Ah, *buona sera*, Signora Tolle.' She surprised Lexi by recognising her on sight. 'Your husband is sleeping but you must go in and sit with him,' she invited. 'He will be more comfortable once he knows you are here.'

Lexi walked across the room towards the door the nurse had indicated. Her heart was thumping, beating like a drum in her ears. She pushed open the door, stepped through it, then swiftly closed it behind her so she could lean back against it, light-headed with fear of what she was about to see.

The room was bigger than the one she'd stayed in. A large white cube of space, shrouded by soft striped shadows cast by the slatted blinds angled against the golden light of the afternoon sun. And she could feel every pore absorbing the hush of perfect stillness as she stood glued to the spot by the sight of the drips and tubes leading to a monitor alive with graphs and numbers that silently flickered and pulsed.

'You can come closer, Lexi. I won't bite.'

# CHAPTER TWO

THE sound of that dry, slightly hoarse voice ran through Lexi in shivering stings of sharp recognition and she dropped her gaze to the bed, unaware that she'd been avoiding it in fear of what she was going to see.

She discovered that she could not see anything other than a swathe of starched white linen. She saw no pillows, and a cage had been erected over his legs. Her wildly skipping heart suddenly felt all curled up in her chest, cowering, as if something was threatening it. For when someone was forced to lie flat it usually meant a back injury. A cage usually meant broken legs. And whatever those tubes were feeding into him made her squirm, because she hadn't bothered to ask anyone what his injuries were. Not the nurse, not Pietro… Perhaps she should go back out there and—

'Lexi…' Franco murmured impatiently when she took too long to answer him. 'If you are thinking of making a quick exit—don't.'

'H-how did you know it was me?' she asked.

'You still wear the same perfume.'

She was surprised he remembered, bearing in mind the trail of different perfumes that had passed through his life since her. Dozens of women listed in celebrity magazines. All smooth, sleek, sophisticated, with—

'Since I cannot move, have some pity on me, *cara*. Come over here where I can see you, *per favore*.'

Curling taut fingers around the shoulder strap of her bag, Lexi peeled herself free of the door and walked forward on limbs that shook. Pulling to a halt at the foot of the bed, she felt her hectic breathing dry up altogether when she got her first glimpse of Franco's powerful length, laid out flat on the bed like a corpse. A white linen sheet covered three-quarters of him—his upper torso left uncovered to reveal the muscled solidity of his wide shoulders and arms like a splash of polished bronze against the starched white. White bandaging formed heavy strapping around his left shoulder and bound his ribs, and she gulped as a wave of distress broke through her when she caught sight of the dark, inky bruising spreading out from beneath the edges of the strapping.

'*Ciao,*' he murmured, in a husky low tone that sounded scraped.

Lexi gave a helpless shake of her head as her eyes began to sting with hot aching tears. 'Just look at the state of you,' she whispered.

Franco did not care that he was really pleased to see the evidence of those tears appear like deep pools in her beautiful eyes. He *wanted* Lexi to be upset. He even wanted her to pity him—was in fact ready and willing to push her sympathy buttons for all they were worth.

*Dio mio,* she looked good, he thought as he lay there waiting for her to look directly into his face. Her hair floated around her slender shoulders like a burnished halo, framing the exquisite triangle of her face with its wide spaced eyes and cute little nose and pointed chin. He did not care that she was pressing her soft lips together in a failed attempt to stop them from trembling, or that the grey patterned scarf she wore looped around her neck was as unflatteringly drab as the grey jacket she was wearing, which hid away from him all that he knew was softly curvy and gracefully sleek. For him she was still his first glimmer of sunlight in the darkest days of his life.

'Look at me,' he urged, feeling her fierce tension throb between them like an extra heartbeat. He could feel the fight she was waging with herself over allowing her eyes to make contact with his, and he understood why it was a fight. Once upon a time they hadn't been able to look at each other without wanting to devour each other. When they'd stopped looking their whole fated relationship had gone into an acute downward slide.

'Please, *cara*,' he husked, then watched as her eyelashes fluttered, the long dusky crescents rising upwards to reveal the depth of the ocean swirled by a hundred different emotions; that caused a clutch of agony so deep inside him the machine behind him started bleeping like mad.

Lexi shot a startled look at it, her breath lurching free from her strangled throat. Things were happening. She hadn't a clue what a normal pulse or blood pressure should read, but the flickering numbers on that machine were rising fast, and it scared her enough to send her shooting round the edge of the bed.

'What's wrong?' She reached for his hand where it lay on the bed, only to stare down in horror when she found herself clutching hold of a plastic shunt with tubes coming out of it. But before she could snatch her hand away Franco turned his hand over and imprisoned hers inside his warm, surprisingly strong grip.

'I'm OK,' he said, without enough strength to convey confidence.

The door suddenly flew open and the nurse swept in. With a brief vague smile at Lexi, she went around to the other side of the bed and began checking things.

'I think your wife must have surprised you.'

Lexi translated the nurse's smiling tease from Italian to English.

'She did *something* to me anyway,' Franco returned ruefully.

Catching onto his meaning, Lexi tried to reclaim her fingers but Franco just tightened his grip, and after a second or so compassion took over and she let her fingers relax in his. The moment she did so he closed his eyes and inched out a very controlled sigh. Almost immediately the number readings began to ease downwards. Flanking each side of the bed, the nurse and Lexi watched the monitor—the nurse with her fingers lightly circling his wrist, Lexi with her fingers still enclosed by his.

By the time everything seemed to have gone back to normal Lexi felt so weak she reached out with her free hand for the chair positioned to her right, drew it closer to the bed and sat down.

Franco didn't move or open his eyes, and as the room slowly settled back into quiet stillness, Lexi let herself look at his face again. She was instantly drenched by the old fierce magnetism that had always been her downfall where Franco was concerned.

He was, quite simply, breathtakingly handsome. There wasn't even a cut or a bruise to distort the sheer quality of masculine perfection stamped into that face. Working at a theatrical agency had, she'd thought, made her immune to so much male beauty, because she dealt with handsome men on a day-to-day basis. But everything about this man set her own blood pressure rising, she acknowledged helplessly—soaking up every small detail while he lay there, unaware of her scrutiny. The smooth, high and intelligent brow below ebony hair cropped short to tame its desire to curl. The subtle arch of his eyebrows above heavy eyelids tipped with eyelashes so long they rested against the slanting planes of his cheekbones. Half of his blood was pure Roman on his mother's side, and the line of his long, only slightly hooked nose, gave credence to that; while the wide, sensual contours of his well shaped mouth belonged to his proud Ligurian father.

Though right now that mouth was pressed shut and the corners turned down a little due to the pain he must be suffering, the agony of overwhelming grief.

'I'm so very sorry about Marco,' she murmured painfully.

Instantly the machine started beeping again. The nurse sent Lexi a sharp frowning glance, then added a faint shake of her head to convey the message that Franco was not ready to talk about Marco.

Her own lips pinching together in an effort to control a painful surge of understanding, Lexi looked back at Franco. A stark greyish tint had settled like a veil across his face, and she knew he was looking that way because he was blaming himself for Marco's death. Where Franco led Marco always followed. Anyone who knew the two friends knew that. But the slavelike loyalty Marco had bestowed on Franco had been both flattering and a burden—as Lexi knew only too well, since she had enslaved herself to him in the same way. And look at the burden *she* had become.

Was that the reason she had come here? Because she knew her slavish love and total dependency on him had become a terrible burden and she now felt guilty about that?

Right there, Lexi fell back in to that long summer four years ago when, at nineteen years old, she had finally done something all by herself after years of being sheltered by her over protective mother, Grace—beautiful Grace Hamilton, who'd sacrificed her own acting career to manage her daughter's surprise rise to fame.

But the year Lexi was nineteen Grace had fallen in love for the first time in her life and married Philippe Reynard, a French entrepreneur with all the outward trappings of celebrity and wealth so yearned for by Grace. He'd owned a fancy apartment in Paris and a rambling château in Bordeaux; and a yacht on which he'd spent most of his summers. He'd made

Grace feel like a princess, and encouraged her to loosen the chains on her daughter so that the two of them could enjoy an extended honeymoon sailing around the Greek Islands on his yacht.

Lexi had been allowed to travel to the Cannes Film Festival without her mother playing strict chaperone.

Excited about striking out on her own for the first time in her life, she had let the freedom go straight to her head and she had become sucked into the glamorous high life. She had proceeded to live it with the destructive blindness of a junkie—until it had been over her ability to think straight about anything…especially what she was doing to herself.

From Cannes to Nice, Cap Ferrat, Monte Carlo, San Remo—

San Remo…

Lexi closed her eyes and saw the same radiant blue skies and glistening waters she'd seen on the television screen. She saw the rows of fancy yachts berthed in exclusive marinas, the stylish boulevards lined with fashionable designer shops, and the pavement café bars frequented by the spoiled offspring of outrageous wealth. Places for the golden people to hang out, with their golden skins and golden smiles and glittering golden futures already mapped out for them. She could hear the golden ring of their laughter—feel the wildly seductive tug of their totally unflappable self-belief. When they'd allowed her entry into their select assembly she'd truly believed that she was one of them—the current golden girl of movie fame.

And of course there'd been Franco, the most golden of them all. The one possessed of all the male beauty his richly aristocratic Italian heritage could bestow. Older than her, so much more experienced than her, the leader of the pack of those super-exclusives. And she'd caught him. She, little Miss Totally-Naïve-and-Sheltered, had won the jewel in the crown without bothering to question how she had done it. Not once had it occurred to her that her new friends had found her na-ivety hilarious—a novelty worthy of turning into a highly entertaining game.

Lexi shivered as the cold, cold truth of her complete humiliation simultaneously creeped up her and chilled her to the bone.

Six months after it had all started it was over—the wreck of her life floundering amongst the wreckage of so much more destruction. Her mother and her new stepfather killed in a freak car accident. The shattering discovery that Philippe Reynard had lived his whole life in hock and, during his short marriage to her mother, had neatly and cleanly stripped Grace of all the money Lexi had earned until there was none of it left.

He'd called it 'investing in Lexi's future.' What a sick joke.

And even all that was not what had dropped her into the lowest, darkest place to which she had ever sunk. No. Her pale face was pinched as she stared at the man who had taken over her life. Lexi recalled the other damning piece of information that had really shattered her. She'd finally learned about the bet her new friends had placed to see which male ego would relieve her of her so obvious innocence before the end of that golden summer. She'd learned about the way all those people she'd stupidly called friends had watched and wagered and eventually laughed their exclusive heads off when Franco had won the prize. If she lived to be a hundred she would never be able to blank out the video someone had sent to her phone of Franco collecting his winnings. She still saw the date, the time and his lazily complacent smile. The only thing missing had been photographic evidence that he had actually bedded her. But that did not mean such evidence had not been around. Once the veils had been ripped from her eyes about Franco, she'd been able to believe him capable of anything. She'd been nothing but a big joke to him, and when the joke had backfired he had not known how the hell to cope.

In the way fate had of balancing things out, Francesco Tolle, golden boy of Europe's glittering society, had found himself punished for his callous treatment of her when she'd found herself orphaned, pregnant and broke.

Lexi blinked back to the present as a door closed, and she realised the nurse had left them alone. Looking back at the monitor, she saw that everything had settled back down again while she'd been taking a walk down memory lane.

Franco still did not open his eyes, and Lexi began to wonder if he'd fallen asleep. She looked down at their hands still clasped together, his long strong fingers totally engulfing hers in the same way they'd used to do—only without the worrying shunt piercing the back of his hand, feeding liquids and drugs into his veins.

Hands that knew her more intimately than any other pair of hands, she thought, shifting on the chair when the thought became a physical memory that skittered across the surface of her skin. Lexi frowned, annoyed with herself for being so susceptible to a mere memory. It wasn't as though he had the smooth caressing hands of an office dweller. His were firm, slightly callused capable hands, because Franco was at his happiest when he was hauling sail ropes on his yacht, *Miranda*, which he'd lived on that summer—or covered in grease and grime taking a boat engine to bits before he painstakingly put it back together again. Franco was a mariner through to his soul. Sailboats, powerboats, natty fast speedboats—even the giant supertankers and cruise liners the Tolle shipyard constructed near Livorno. As a qualified marine engineer Franco was in his element, no matter what size the craft. That he could also be successful at the business end of the Tolle empire was an extra string to his talented bow.

Then there was his well documented success with women. And why not? Lexi thought, unable to stop drifting her eyes over his powerful form, most of which was now hidden beneath the sheet. Leonardo da Vinci would have loved to meet Franco, she decided, for he *was* his 'Vitruvian Man.' Everything about him was in perfect proportion—even the strength reflected in his squared chin. He badly needed a shave, she noticed, feeling her fingers start to tingle with an urge to run them over the rough shadow that gave him the look of a reckless buccaneer. That he was—reckless, anyway; or he would not enjoy racing a supercharged powerboat at such dangerous speeds.

It was no wonder she'd fallen for him like an adolescent, dazzled by his larger than life personality. Physically he was every woman's secret fantasy man, complete with that other vital ingredient—a powerfully magnetic sexual virility. It radiated from him even as he lay there, bruised and weakened.

Lexi tugged in a small breath, overcome by the desire to stroke her fingers over the rest of him, let her senses reconnect with all that glorious male beauty laid out in front of her like a sacrifice. As a lover he'd been wildly exciting—the kind of lover who loved to be stroked and petted as much as he loved to do both. As a companion he'd possessed enough lazy charm and captivating charisma to blind her to all his faults.

He was kind to old ladies and animals. He could laugh without constraint at the absurd, and—all the more potent—he could laugh at himself. He had a brilliant technical brain that had allowed him to design and build his first sailing yacht at the age of thirteen. He was super-confident and totally fearless when it came to any sport that took place on water. And he could lie in the sun for hours without moving. Relaxing for Franco was as important as competing in some crazy sport or his other favoured pastime: sex. Long afternoons and nights of deeply sensual, stunningly uninhibited loving was the sweet honey that gave him his boundless energy.

And he could be cruel enough and ruthless enough to take on a bet to seduce the naive interloper in his circle of elite friends because he liked to be challenged and he liked to win—to hell with the cost to the targeted victim.

Something else swept through Lexi. It was the rumbling of a hurt she had buried so deep it still had not worked its way back to the surface—though she was letting herself remember all the things she had shut away with that hurt. Things like the hard clench of dismay on his face when she'd broken the news to him that she was pregnant. The change in his eyes, as if someone had splashed the warm brown iris with a glaze of ice. Then there was the quiet sombre way he'd taken responsibility for his mistake and ultimately taken responsibility for her.

Where had her pride been when she'd let him do that? Smothered, by blind love and the desperate fear of losing him. Lexi was ashamed of that. But she felt more ashamed knowing that, for all the unforgivable things Franco had done to her all those years ago, she'd more or less walked into marriage with him to punish him for that ugly, humiliating bet.

And maybe that was the reason why she had come here—because she'd always known deep down that she had behaved no better than Franco had.

Looking up, she collided full on with a pair of stunning dark eyes the multicolours of tiger's-eye quartz. Yet another heated flush flared through her body, leaving her feeling stripped bare and exposed. Because she knew him. She knew by his carefully impassive expression that he'd been lying there so still because he had been reading her every thought as it had passed across her face.

Pulling her hand free of his grasp, she sat back in her chair, tense now and skittish. 'I don't know why I've come here,' she confessed in a helpless rush, laying something else bare for him: the battles she'd been having with herself.

Franco wished he did not feel so damn weak. There were tears in her eyes again, though she was trying her best to fight them. And her hair was catching the sunlight streaming in through the slatted blinds, setting it on fire with a thousand different shades of gold and red.

'I had this h-horrible premonition you were going to die, and if I didn't come I would always regret being so m-mean to you.'

'Would it help you to feel better if I complied with your premonition, *cara*?' he offered flatly. 'It would make you a rich widow, at all events.'

'Don't talk like that.' Lexi speared him with a pained look. 'I never wished you dead and I don't want your money.'

'I know you don't—which makes this situation all the more ironic.'

Ironic? 'Where is the irony in you lying here all battered and broken?'

'I am not in as bad a condition as I look.' The quiet assurance sent her restless gaze tracking over him once again.

'Explain your definition of a not bad condition.' She waved a trembling hand to encompass all the evidence in front of her, including the computerised machine monitoring him as well as feeding all sorts of drugs into him via the shunt in the back of his hand. 'You're lying fl—flat on your back and you've got a cage over your legs.'

'I am lying flat as a mere precaution, because I wrenched a couple of vertebra and the only thing wrong with my legs is a gash to my left thigh, which had to be stitched up.'

Her restless eyes moved to his bound chest. 'And all that strapping?'

'A couple of cracked ribs and a dislocated shoulder they had a fight manipulating back into place.'

She went pale as her tummy churned squeamishly at the image he'd just placed in her head. 'Anything else?' she squeezed out.

'A sore head?' he offered up.

A sore head... No broken bones, then. No crushing brain damage. No life-threatening injury to justify his father's insistence that she come here... Lexi lurched out from the strains of anxiety to embrace the sting of annoyance in the single release of her breath. 'You're supposed to be seriously ill,' she said accusingly.

'You don't see these injuries as serious?'

'No.' The summer she'd met Franco he had been cruising the Mediterranean while convalescing after breaking a leg so badly he'd required several surgeries and countless metal pins to get the leg to mend. 'Your father gave me the impression that you—'

'Wanted to see you?'

'Bleeding and broken and asking for me!' She quoted Salvatore. 'That implied you were in a coma or s-something.'

'People in comas don't speak—'

'Oh, shut up.' Jumping to her feet, Lexi paced restlessly away from the bed—only to swing right back again. 'Why did you want to see me?'

The heavy veil of his eyelids lowered to screen his thoughts. 'Lose the bag and take the jacket and scarf off before you roast.'

'I'm not stopping,' Lexi countered edgily.

'You're stopping,' he contended, 'because you took one look at me and now you can't help yourself staying around to keep on looking.'

She dragged in a strangled breath. 'Of all the conceited—' Fiercely she breathed out again.

'Dio mio,' he ground out. 'Even as I am lying here injured and in pain, and pretty damn helpless, you could not resist mentally stripping me of the covers so you could reacquaint yourself with what I look like.'

'That's not true!' Lexi denied hotly.

He just smiled the smile of a cat who'd cornered the mouse. 'I might be physically flattened, but all my other faculties are in good working order. I know when I'm being lusted after.

You look sensational too, *bella mia,*' he diverted smoothly. 'Even trussed up in all those clothes you've got on.'

'It's cold in England.' Why she'd said that Lexi didn't have a single clue.

'Glad I didn't make it there, then,' Franco responded. 'September should be a glorious month. English weather has lost its good taste…'

He closed his eyelids all the way now, as if he didn't have the strength to hold them up any longer. Lexi chewed on her bottom lip for a few seconds, wondering what she should do next.

'You're tired,' she murmured. 'You should rest…'

'I am resting.'

'Yes, but…' She slid a restless glance over him again. 'I should leave you to do it in peace.'

Irritation tightened his facial muscles. 'You have only just arrived here.'

'I know…' She was uncomfortably aware that she had moved back to the side of the bed. 'But you know you don't really need me here, Franco. It's just—'

'I was going to come to London to see you after the race, then—this happened.' The impatient flick of his unencumbered hand adequately relayed what *this* was. 'There are things we need to talk about.'

None that Lexi could bring to mind, except— A sound of thickened horror broke free from her throat. 'Are you saying it was because I sent you divorce papers that you crashed your boat?'

'No, I am not saying that,' he snapped, then let out a groan, as if even getting angry hurt him.

Lexi's eyes went straight to the monitor. 'You OK?'

*'Si,'* he muttered, but she could see that his breathing had gone shallow, his beautifully shaped mouth drooping with tension. 'Damn ribs kill me every time I breathe.'

'And you look ready to pass out,' Lexi said anxiously, watching the grey pallor wash across his face again.

'It's the drugs. I will be free of them by tomorrow, then I can get out of here.'

About to remark on that overconfident statement, she held back because she could tell he was only voicing wishful thoughts.

A silence fell between them. After shifting from one foot to the other a couple of times, Lexi gave in to what she really wanted to do, but didn't really want to do, sit down again. It was exhausting to be locked in this constant battle with herself, she admitted as she sat watching his breathing become less shallow and the tension in his face relax.

She just wished he didn't look so achingly vulnerable, because that didn't help her at all. Nor did it help when an old memory slunk into her head, showing her a moment—a short space in time in their hostile marriage—when Franco had sat beside her bed all night long. They'd had a horrid row, she recalled. Just another one of many rows—but this one had ended with her spinning away to walk out of the room, only to end up dropping at his feet in a faint. She must have been out for ages, because when she'd eventually come round she'd been in her bed and a doctor was leaning over her, gravely viewing the blood pressure band he had strapped around her arm.

Glancing up at the flashy screen that was monitoring Franco's vital statistics, she grimaced. His must be scoring an OK blood pressure because the thing wasn't beeping, whereas the old fashioned version she'd felt squeezing her arm had given her no clue at all that her pressure was a cause for concern.

She looked back at Franco. His hair had gone curly, she noticed for the first time. If he knew he would be mad. Franco went to great expense to make sure his hair didn't show its natural tendency to curl. His hair had been curly the night she'd fainted. He'd stood like some brooding dark statue at the end of her bed but it was only now, looking back, that she remembered the ruffled curly hair and the same grey cast to his face that had been swimming over it today.

'Your wife needs rest and no stress, Signor Tolle,' the doctor had informed him. 'I will come back in the morning.' He'd then spoken to Lexi herself. 'If your blood pressure has not fallen by then you will be going into hospital.' It had been both a warning and a threat.

'I'm sorry.'

Lexi blinked, because that gruff apology had sounded in her head as if Franco had only just said it.

'Go away and leave me alone,' she'd told him, and turned her back to him.

He hadn't gone away. They say that misery loves company, and it had certainly been true for the two of them that long and miserable night, when he'd pulled up an armchair and sat in it, a grimly silent figure in the darkness, watching over her.

Sliding back into the present, Lexi was surprised to discover that the room had slowly darkened while she'd been sitting there, lost in her memories. Franco still had not moved so much as a glossy black eyelash as far as she could tell.

What was it they had been arguing about? She couldn't remember, though it was likely she'd been the one who started it—she usually had. When love turned to hate it was a cold, bitter kind of hatred, she'd discovered. The target for your hatred could not do or say anything right.

Good time to make your silent exit, Lexi, she told herself—not wanting to feel like the person she had turned into back then. Stooping down to pick up her bag from where she'd placed it on the floor, she rose to her feet and turned towards the door.

'Where are you going?' Franco murmured.

Surprise stung down her spinal cord. 'I thought I'd go now and let you sleep.'

'If I promise to fall into a deep coma will you stay?'

Lexi swung back round. 'That wasn't even remotely funny, Francesco!'

Through the gloom she saw his mouth stretch into a mocking kind of grimace, 'You sound like a really snappy wife.'

'And that was even less funny, considering my track record in that particular role.' She sighed heavily.

'And I was the selfish husband from hell.'

Yes, well, she had no argument with either assessment. Neither of them had been any good at being married. Great at being lovers—warm and carefree, fabulously imaginative and gloriously passionate lovers—but as for the rest...

'Listen... ' She heaved a deep, fortifying breath. 'I hope you get better soon. And I am truly sorry about—about Marco.' She had to say it, even though the nurse had indicated that Franco wasn't ready to talk about his best friend. 'But you must know as well as I do that I don't belong here.'

'I want you here,' he stated grimly.

Lexi shook her head. 'You're going to be OK. In a couple of days you'll be wondering why you wanted me to come here at all.'

'I know exactly why I want you here.'

Ignoring that, 'I'm going back to London,' she said.

'Go through that door and I will pull out these tubes and come right after you, Lexi,' Franco warned her flatly.

She uttered yet another sigh. 'Why would you want to do something as stupid as that?'

'I told you.' The line of his mouth was severely compressed now, 'We need to talk.'

'We can talk through our lawyers.' Lexi continued determinedly towards the door.

'You will have this particular talk to my face, *cara*, because I don't want a divorce.'

She swung round yet again. 'Until today we haven't so much as spoken a word or set eyes on each other for three and a half years!' Lexi reminded him. 'Of course you want a divorce. I want a divorce.'

That said, she turned and reached for the door handle, heard a sound from behind her that sent a cold chill racing down her spine, and spun right back to discover that Franco was sitting up and attempting to pluck out the shunt from his hand. But his coordination was obviously wrecked by the drugs.

'What do you think you are you doing?' Shrieking alarm sent Lexi darting back to the bed to cover his hand and the shunt with her both of her own hands in an effort to stop him, but he just changed tack and threw back the covering sheet instead. Even as she tried to grab it the cage went flying onto the floor. The next shock wave hit her when she saw for the first time what the cage and sheet had been covering up. More bandaging strapped one powerfully structured thigh, but it wasn't that that shocked. Even in the gloom she could see the sickening extent of his bruising, which spread right the way down his left side.

'Oh, my God,' she choked, fighting to wrest the sheet from him at the same time as she tried to block him from getting up off the bed. The beeps and alarms started sounding like crazy. Reacting as if programmed to do it without thinking, Lexi reached out and took Franco's face between her palms, made him look at her.

'Please stop it,' she begged, then, because he looked so totally hurt and stubborn, she bent her head and crushed her trembling lips against his.

She kissed him without understanding why she kissed him. And she continued to kiss him even after Franco stopped fighting and went perfectly, perfectly still. It was like her own moment of madness: she didn't even stop when bright lights were suddenly blazing and the nurse was letting out a sharp gasp of shock. The alarms played a riotous symphony in harmony with the stirring mud of long subdued pleasures that split open huge fissures across her aching heart.

When she did eventually pull away she was breathing fast. She felt his fast breath feather her face and looked into eyes turned to stunning black-onyx. Tears gathered—hot tears, pained tears—and she was trembling.

'I'll stay,' she shook out thickly and brokenly. 'I will do anything so long as you lie down again. Please, Franco. Please, I will stay...'

# CHAPTER THREE

LEXI sat in one of the chairs in the anteroom beside Franco's room and clutched the hot cup of coffee the nurse had just pressed on her, while a white coated man who had introduced himself as Dr Cavelli sat beside her, waiting for her violent shivers to stop.

She was in shock. She still couldn't take on board what she had done. Her lips burned and felt swollen. Tears smarted her eyes; she was still feeling the buzzing effects of the fear and panic she'd felt when she'd seen Franco trying to get up off the bed. If she had not witnessed it for herself she would never have believed that he could behave in such an irrational way. For a man basically made up of one big bruise, he'd displayed shockingly phenomenal brute strength.

'You have to understand, Signora Tolle—' Dr Cavelli spoke gently '—your husband does not require twenty-four hour nursing surveillance because his physical injuries require such intensive monitoring. It is his mental state which concerns us the most.'

Lifting her head up, Lexi repeated, 'His mental state?' with a strangled breath of disbelief.

'Overall, your husband is exceptionally strong and healthy—as he has just demonstrated.' The glimmer of a rueful smile touched Dr Cavelli's lips. 'His physical injuries are many, but already they are beginning to heal. However, he has recently lost his closest friend in violent circumstances, and his feelings of shock and grief are great.'

'Franco and Marco were like twin brothers.' Lexi nodded in bleak understanding. 'Of course he's feeling Marco's loss very deeply.'

'It is the way he is dealing with that loss that concerns us. As I believe you have already witnessed, if Signor Clemente's name is mentioned your husband either ignores the subject or becomes—agitated.'

'Of course he becomes agitated.' Lexi fired up in Franco's defence. 'How would you prefer him to react? Fall into a fit of weeping? He's a man. He's in shock and he's injured. He must be suffering terrible feelings of guilt because he survived when Marco did not, and—'

'*Signora*, that is the point I am trying to make,' Dr Cavelli intruded. 'Men and women react to extreme stress differently. A woman generally vents her distress in some way.'

Recalling the way she'd just kissed Franco, Lexi dipped her eyes from the watchful doctor's as a heated blush surged through her face.

'A typical male's response, however, is to protect himself by detaching himself from the tragedy. He blocks it out.'

'He just needs time to—recover a little.' Lexi leapt once again to Franco's defence. 'The accident only happened this morning, but already you're telling me he's on some kind of suicide watch!'

Franco suicidal? Were they all mad?

'I don't think I used quite such dramatic language,' the doctor protested distractedly.

Glowering at him—because what he'd said had been very dramatic to *her* way of thinking—Lexi was disconcerted to find that he was studying her from beneath a seriously puzzled frown, and there was an extra throb in the tension surrounding them that made her glance at the nurse, who was back at her station. She saw that she was staring oddly at her too.

'What?' she demanded sharply. 'What have I said to make you look at me like that?' Prickling with alarm all over again, Lexi set down the coffee before she spilled it. 'He hasn't attempted to—?'

Dr Cavelli gave a quick shake of his head to dispense with that fear. '*Signora*…the accident took place three days ago.'

Lexi blinked. What was he talking about? 'But I saw it on the news today,' she insisted, 'It said…' But she couldn't remember if it had given an actual time or a date. 'And Franco's father only called me this morning—'

'Your husband has been drifting in and out of consciousness for two days and only regained full consciousness this morning.'

Lexi continued to stare at him, feeling a bit like an owl perched on a branch that she was in danger of tumbling off. Twitter. She'd heard Suzy talking about Twitter. Her inner vision glanced back at the fifty-inch flat screen and recalled for the first time that they must have been watching one of those news review channels—the kind that loved reporting gory crashes and…

Laying her fingers across her mouth, she started to shake again. Franco had been lying there injured for three days and she'd known nothing about it. She—

'His agitation erupted almost as soon as he woke up,' the doctor continued. 'He refused to let us speak of Signor Clemente once his father had broken the news of his friend's death. He had his room cleared of the flowers and cards he had received from family and friends. He banned those same people from entering this hospital to visit him.'

For the first time since she'd arrived there Lexi glanced around the quiet anteroom and took in the distinct lack of friends and family she should have expected to see crowded in there.

'Wh—Where is Franco's father?' she whispered.

'Signor Salvatore Tolle is on your husband's banned list, Signora,' the doctor informed her.

Eyes rounding like saucers, Lexi gasped. 'Are you kidding me?'

Dr Cavelli shook his head. 'Your husband is very angry with the world right now. It is not unusual for such tragic circumstances to make people angry,' he assured her. 'However, when he demanded to see you and his father explained that you had not been contacted he—reacted badly. He attempted to get out of his bed, insisting he was going to London to see you. The depth of his agitation concerned us enough to suggest to his father that he contact you and bring you here as quickly as he could. Once your husband knew you were on your way here he calmed down a little.'

But when she'd tried to leave again he'd pulled the same mad stunt!

'What we believe has happened is, to help him to block out his natural grief and guilt with regard to Signor Clemente's death, he has transferred his full focus to you and the—forgive me—the state of your marriage.'

The divorce papers. Lexi closed her eyes tightly as her heart sank and the clamouring sickness she felt began to churn up her stomach. Franco had crashed his boat because he'd been thinking of those papers instead of concentrating on—

*No.* Pushing trembling, tense fingers through her hair, Lexi gave a fierce shake of her head, refusing to believe that the arrival of divorce papers had had the power to tip Franco over the edge.

'Our marriage has been over for three and a half years,' she mumbled, more to herself than to anyone else. She just couldn't bring herself to consider that he would react so badly to something he must have been expecting—or even been thinking of putting into motion himself!

What Franco had seemingly done was to transfer his focus onto the divorce papers *after* the accident, Lexi decided. Though she couldn't work out why he should want to use that particular thing to focus on.

'I'll go and talk to him,' she said, getting to her feet. 'He can't possibly have meant to ban his own father from his bedside. I'll go and find out why he's behaving like this and—'

'He is sleeping, *signora*,' the doctor reminded her as she turned towards Franco's door. 'Perhaps it would be wiser for you to sleep on what we have discussed before you talk to him again.'

It had not been a suggestion but a carefully worded command, and it spun Lexi about. Her eyes flashed out vivid blue warnings—she knew because she could feel them doing it. 'He isn't at death's door,' she stated bluntly. 'Neither is he a child to be cosseted and protected from the truth. And the truth is it's just not fair of him to take his feelings out on his father.'

'Perhaps by tomorrow you will have calmed down a little and thought better of…challenging him right now.'

'What kind of doctor are you?' she demanded, suddenly suspicious.

'The kind that deals with a patient's mental health,' he provided, with a small, tellingly dry smile. 'Your husband's injuries are many, *signora*. In no way would I like to think I had given you the impression that we undervalue his physical trauma, because we do not. His heart stopped beating twice at the scene of the accident. The trauma team had to fight to bring him back. His concussion was and still is very concerning—he has clouded vision and continued dizziness…'

Lexi blinked as she recalled the way Franco's hand had kept on missing its target when it tried to pull out the shunt.

'The wound in his thigh was deep and required several hours of careful surgery to reconnect vital nerves and muscles.' As Lexi went pale, Dr Cavelli spread out his hands in an expression of apology for being so graphic. 'Extensive internal bleeding required us to insert a drain in his chest cavity—I should imagine you saw the resulting spread of bruising,' he gauged. 'The loss of blood was significant enough to require several urgent transfusions, and we feared for a time—unnecessarily, we now know—that he had damaged his spinal cord as well. I tell you all of this because I believe facing him with questions about the way he is dealing with his current situation might goad him into doing something more drastic than attempting to get out of bed—like walking out of here altogether.'

'Does he have the strength to do that?' Lexi questioned dubiously.

'He has the determination and will power to give him the strength,' the doctor assessed, and, thinking about it, Lexi conceded that he was probably right. 'Your husband has made you the linchpin which is holding him together right now. Therefore I must beg you most seriously to consider the responsibility this places on you to help him through this very difficult time…'

'You lied to me about the extent of your injuries,' Lexi said the moment Franco opened his eyes.

It was very late, and she'd ignored the doctor's advice and come back here to sit with Franco while he slept.

'And you can't banish your father from your bedside unless you want to break his heart,' she tagged on. 'Why would Salvatore think of calling me and bringing me over here? It isn't as if you and I are friends, is it?'

The moment she saw the grey cast settle over his face Lexi recognised her mistake. Mentioning friends had reminded him of Marco, and, as the doctor had described, Franco had blocked her words out.

She heaved out a tense little breath. 'OK.' She tried a different tack. 'You can't keep trying to get out of this bed either. Not until they say that you can.'

'Are you staying?'

Remembering that kiss, and her subsequent promise, Lexi shifted tensely. 'I told you I was staying.'

'Tell me again so I can be sure, and this time make it a promise.'

'Franco,' she sighed out wearily, 'this is all so...'

At was as if something or someone had switched her off. Franco watched her frown and catch her bottom lip with her teeth. He took in the loss of colour in her cheeks and the signs of strain and exhaustion bruising the circles around her eyes. The slight quiver in the lip she was biting told him she was upset, and the way she had to think before she spoke told him she had been gagged by the doctor from saying what she really wanted to say to him.

Lexi was stubborn. She was not the emotional pushover everyone liked to think she was. She had a hot, impulsive temper and right now he could tell she was having a fight to keep that temper in check, because he had, in effect, chained her to this bed with him.

Did he feel bad about that? No, he felt bloody elated about that. They'd gagged her and he'd chained her to his bed. All he wanted right now was for her to confirm that.

'OK.' She heaved in a fresh lungful of air. 'I promise to stay around.'

'Then I will not try to get out of this bed until they say that I can,' he parried, and turned his hand over on the white sheet, watching as she looked down at it, knowing that she understood what the gesture meant. After a short hesitation she lifted her own hand and placed it against his.

Deal sealed, he thought as he folded his fingers around her fingers, then released a sigh of contentment and closed his eyes. 'What time is it?' he asked.

'Ten o'clock,' Lexi answered. 'You slept through dinner—'

'I'm not hungry.'

'—so I ate it,' she concluded.

That brought his eyes back open, and placed a lazy smile on his lips. He turned his head to look at her and his eyes had softened. That awful blank glaze had gone to reveal deep brown irises like velvet threaded with gold that warmed her all the way through even though she did not want it to.

'What was it?' he questioned curiously.

'*Pomodori con riso* supplied by Zeta,' she told him. 'Your father has arranged for her to—'

'Did she send a dessert?'

He'd done it again—blocked her from mentioning his father. 'A couple of truly delicious Maritozzi buns. Franco, about your father—'

He withdrew his hands from hers. 'Since when have you been Salvatore's biggest fan?' he demanded impatiently. 'He treated you like a lowlife when we were together.'

'I'm not his adored son.'

Flattening out his lips, he shut his eyes again.

In bubbling frustration Lexi sat back in her seat, then instantly sat forward again: no matter what the doctor had advised, or what Franco himself preferred, she found she still could not let the subject rest.

She reached out to retrieve his hand. 'Francesco, please just listen—'

'Franco,' he interrupted. 'I know you are mad with me when you call me Francesco.'

Lowering her gaze to his hand, Lexi watched her own fingers drawing patterns on his palm the way she'd used to do when they talked. Quite suddenly she wanted to break down and weep. They'd been together for six months. For two of those months they had been inseparable. For the other four they'd hated each other's guts.

'And when you extend that to Francesco Tolle,' he continued, giving a good mimic of her cut-crystal English accent, 'I know I am in really deep trouble.'

'You stopped calling me Lexi altogether,' Lexi recalled dully. 'I became Alexia—and if you think *my* accent was cold, yours was made of ice picks.'

'I was angry.'

'I know you were.'

'I was wildly in love with you but we—'

She stood up so fast Franco had no chance to react. By the time he'd dragged his heavy eyelids open it was like looking at a stranger—an achingly beautiful but distant stranger.

'I'd better be going. I need to find somewhere to stay.'

'Pietro will have reserved a suite for you at a hotel close to the hospital.' Aware that he was slurring his words now, as the drugs they'd fed into him began to drag him back down, Franco decided to let her escape. 'He will be waiting to drive you there.'

'I'll see you tomorrow,' she mumbled, and was gone before he could say anything else.

Releasing a sigh, Franco let his eyelids droop again and saw the other Lexi. The younger one, sitting cross-legged on the bulkhead of his sailing yacht, *Miranda*, relaying some convoluted story to him about an incident that had happened on the film set of the movie she'd come to Cannes to promote. She hadn't had a clue that she was blocking his view of the open sea in front of them. She hadn't cared that a stiff warm breeze was tangling her hair into spiralling knots, or that the tiny red bikini she'd been wearing was revealing more than it should.

And her innocence had shone out of her like a tantalising aura. She'd had no clue that what shone in him was deep, hot and very physical.

She'd liked him.

Franco threw an arm up to cover his eyes and for once wished they'd stung him with more sedatives, because he

did not want to look any harder at the sexual predator he'd
been then. The cabin beneath her, where he'd lived during
that long summer, had already been set up ready for her seduction, and he'd been burning with anticipation while she
talked.

A seduction that had taken them from Cannes to Nice, Cap
Ferrat, Monte Carlo, then San Remo—

San Remo...

Franco shifted onto his side and didn't care that it hurt
him like hell. Reaching for the bell, he waited for the nurse
to come to him. 'I want this cage removed and these tubes
taken out. I want a couple of pillows and I want my mobile
phone,' he reeled off with grim intent.

'But, *signor*—'

'Or I will get up and get them for myself.'

He did not get his first two requests, but he was reluctantly
handed his mobile phone. *'Grazie,'* he murmured, allowing
the nurse to fuss around him, placing the pillows beneath his
shoulders, mainly because he felt too damn weak to do the
job for himself.

Lexi slept like a log. She had not expected to sleep at all,
but the moment her head had come to rest on the pillow exhaustion had taken her out like a light, and she'd awoken this
morning feeling so invigorated, but baffled as to why she
should feel like that.

Or maybe she did not want to look too deeply into why,
she mused with a frown, picking up the phone and ordering
some breakfast, before quickly showering while she waited
for it to arrive. She was starving. Despite telling Franco that
she'd eaten his dinner, she'd been too stressed to do more than
pick at Zeta's delicious dishes. Now her stomach was growl-
ing as she walked across the elegant sitting room of the vast
suite Pietro had reserved for her and went to take a quick look

out of the window to check the weather before deciding what she was going to wear.

Not that her choices were many. Her weekend bag revealed a frustrating lack of common sense when she'd packed it so hastily back in London. Nothing in it was appropriate for hot and sunny Livorno in September; and she discovered she had not even packed any shoes.

A knock sounded on the suite door as she walked out of the bedroom wearing a long-sleeved stripy tunic top and a pair of black leggings tucked into black ankle boots. Assuming Room Service was delivering her breakfast, she opened the door—only to fall back two steps in shock.

There was no mistaking that Franco had been forged in his father's image. Dressed impeccably as always in a dark business suit, and in his mid-fifties, Salvatore Tolle was still a very attractive if dauntingly austere man.

'*Buongiorno*, Alexia,' he greeted her soberly.

'*B-buongiorno, signor,*' she returned in a voice made breathless by surprise.

'May I come in?'

Without saying another word Lexi stepped to one side in silent invitation for him to enter the suite. Nerves made her stay by the door once she'd closed it again. As she watched him take up a stance in the middle of the room she tried to anticipate what his visit could be about.

He took a few moments to glance around her accommodation. 'You are comfortable here?'

She pleated her hands together at her front. 'Yes, of course…thank you.'

He nodded his silver-threaded dark head. 'I have spoken to Francesco,' he announced abruptly. 'He called me last night from his bed.'

'Oh!' Lexi instantly cheered up. 'I'm so glad he did that. I was upset when I heard he had—'

'Your concern on my behalf is touching, but I would prefer

it if you resisted the urge to express it,' Salvatore interrupted in a cool voice.

It felt like having a door slammed shut in her face.

She should be used to it, Lexi told herself. The few conversations she'd ever had with Salvatore had always felt like that.

'Though I *do* thank you, Alexia,' he then surprised her by adding, 'for urging my son to—soften his attitude towards me.'

'N-no problem.' Having been stopped from saying what she would have liked to say to him, Lexi left her response at that.

Another knock sounded on the door, and this time it was her breakfast. Glad of the diversion, because Salvatore had always scared the life out of her, Lexi allowed the waiter entry and watched mutely as he crossed the room to place the tray down on a small table set by the window.

'Can—can I offer you a cup of tea?' she enquired politely, once the waiter had left them again.

'*Grazie*, no,' Salvatore responded. 'However, please—sit down and enjoy your breakfast, ' he insisted.

Lexi sat down at the small table, but the thought of eating or drinking anything in front of him just closed up her throat.

'Please tell me why you're here,' she urged, hearing the strain in her own voice. 'It's not Franco, is it? He hasn't—?'

'Francesco is fine,' came the quick assurance. 'If *fine* accurately describes the injuries he endured,' he added bleakly. 'I have come here directly from visiting with him.'

'Oh, that's…' *Good*, Lexi had been about to say, but held it back by biting down on her tense lower lip.

'Francesco does not know I am here, you understand?' he informed her then. 'He has forbidden me from approaching you, so my relationship with my son is in your hands once again, Alexia.' The rueful smile he offered her almost melted her wariness. 'However, there is a matter I need to discuss with you.'

'Will you at least sit down first?' Feeling pretty uncomfortable sitting there, while he stood tall and straight several metres away, Lexi indicated the vacant chair placed at the table.

He really looked as if he was actually going to take her up on her offer, too; but then he glanced at his wristwatch, frowned, and shook his head. 'I have to leave in a few minutes to catch my flight to New York. We are very close to procuring a large contract there, which will keep our New York shipyard busy for the next four years. Francesco was dealing with the details. Of course now that he cannot I must go in his place...'

Lexi pressed her lips together and nodded her head in understanding. She found she needed something to do with her restless fingers and picked up a glass of juice.

'I must, therefore, ask you to do me another favour,' Salvatore went on. 'Leaving my son without my support at this time is unacceptable. I will be back in time to attend Marco's funeral next week of course,' he assured her quickly, having no idea that she did not already know when Marco's funeral would be. 'However, I will have to return to New York almost immediately afterwards. The thing is, Alexia, all being well, Francesco will be released from hospital in the next few days. Since he has decided to place his complete trust in you, I must ask if you would continue to support him in my place through the coming few weeks.'

Unable to sit still any longer, Lexi got to her feet, feeling very tense now, because she wasn't sure how much of Franco's close company she was going to be able to take without—

'How long are we talking about? I have a job in London, you see, and—and other commitments.'

'I feel that a month's compassionate leave is not too much to ask of your employer.'

He felt that because he didn't know Bruce, thought Lexi, not at all looking forward to *that* conversation.

'Since Francesco is still refusing to allow anyone else to come near him, I am hoping that you will be able to convince him to bypass his apartment here in Livorno and go directly to Monfalcone, where Pietro and Zeta will be on hand to help you with his convalescence.'

He was referring to the private estate just outside Livorno, where she'd stayed during her mess of a brief marriage. Monfalcone was a beautiful *castello* built of golden stone that had mellowed over centuries. It was also the place where she and Franco had been married. A day she would much rather not think back on, because her welcome from the rest of the Tolle family had been so disapproving. In a cold fury Franco had whipped them away from there before the first waltz had been announced and taken her to his apartment in the city for a week. Continuing hostilities between the two of them had prompted a return to Monfalcone, because the *castello* was big enough for the two of them to avoid each other for most of the time.

'He will not go to Monfalcone without you,' Salvatore imparted flatly. 'He is determined to follow you to London if you decide not to stay here. I do not pretend to understand this fixation he has developed about your marriage, but I do know that it is paramount in his thoughts.'

*Guilt*, Lexi wanted to say—but didn't. She'd been thinking about it since she'd left the hospital, and she'd decided that his guilt over Marco's death had stirred up guilty feelings over the way he'd behaved during their short time together as a married couple—though she was not so self-pitying as to think that she had treated him any better than he had treated her.

Every time she'd looked at him she'd seen the lazily complacent smile on his handsome tanned face when he'd accepted his winnings from that rotten bet. Every time he'd made an attempt to mend fences between them, she'd struck out at him like a whip. When he stalked out of the *castello* and hadn't come back for two whole weeks she'd been heartily glad to see the back of him. She'd worn her disillusionment and bitterness like a suit of armour that contained the aching throb of raw, broken-hearted hurt, and she'd hugged it to her for long, lonely months until...

'Am I asking too much of you?'

Without knowing she'd sat down again, Lexi blinked her eyes and realised she been lost in her own thoughts for too long. Looking up at her father-in-law, she saw an expression she never would have expected to see score Salvatore's coldly impassive features. It hinted strongly at despair.

He didn't know what he was going to do if she refused to stay with Franco. Salvatore had a large multinational ship building company to run, whether or not he wanted to go and do it right now.

'I will stay,' she said, and smiled a crooked smile when she counted how many times she'd used those words recently.

# CHAPTER FOUR

LEXI pulled to a stop in the doorway. The monitors had gone, and plump snowy-white pillows now lay stacked on the bed, but there was no Franco resting against them. Swivelling around, she found him seated in a comfortable chair by the window, with a rolling table lowered so it skimmed across his legs, a laptop computer standing open on its top.

'Oh, you're out of bed!' Lexi exclaimed brightly. 'That's great.'

'I am not a kid. Don't talk to me as if I am,' Franco responded, with enough sizzling antagonism to put Lexi on her guard as she stepped further into the room so she could close the door behind her. 'You are late. Where have you been?'

'Sorry, I had some stuff to do.' Dumping her collection of bags down against the wall, she walked over to him. 'When did they let you get up?'

'They didn't *let* me do anything. I got up.'

'Was that wise?'

'I'm still breathing.'

Lexi almost responded with something very sarcastic, then thought better of it and removed her jacket instead. Moving to drape it over a chair, she looked at him again. He was wearing a white bathrobe and nothing else as far she could tell. His hair wore a damp sheen to it, and yesterday's rakish five o'clock shadow had disappeared. So, thankfully, had the sickly pallor from his face. His eyes were veiled, because he was concentrating on the computer screen, and his lips were flattened tight. For Lexi, his manner was a good reminder of what it felt like when Franco turned on his cold side. Words became lethal weapons.

'Well, at least you smell nice anyway,' she murmured idly, determined not to rise to his provoking bait.

A hint of a flash speared out from behind his eyelashes. With the use of only one hand—the strapping around his right shoulder impeded the other—he continued to tap away on the keyboard with a five fingered efficiency that was impressive.

'You left the hotel by taxi at nine o'clock this morning. That was three hours ago. Have you forgotten how to wear a skirt?'

Blinking her eyes at that blunt-ended bombardment, Lexi glanced down at her legs, still encased in stretchy black fabric, and her ankle boots—which were making her feet ache because she'd done too much walking in them and it was too hot outside for boots.

'What kind of skirt would you like me to wear?' she questioned innocently. 'Short and tight? Flared and flirty? Long and floaty?' Strolling back to her bags, she picked them up and hauled them over to the window to dump them down beside his chair, then dropped down into a squat. 'I've bought all three, just in case you have a preference, plus a couple of dresses—mainly because I fell in love with them. Two nighties, some underwear...' As she listed her purchases Lexi scooped the items out of their bags and dropped them on top of his laptop without a single care as to whether she was messing up his five fingered prose. 'It really shocked me what I'd thrown in my case in London because I was in a hurry. I mean, what can a girl *do* with one pair of jeans, no spare tops, no fresh underwear and no shoes?'

He caught the shoes before they landed, his long fingers closing around the pair of strappy flats.

'Oh, and these.' Dipping into a bag, she came out with a clutch of cosmetics and a hairbrush.

'Don't,' he warned softly, when she went to drop them onto his laptop too.

'OK, so you're not impressed with girly necessities. How about this, then...?' Her next dip produced a stuffed pearl-grey floppy-eared rabbit, which she ever so gently laid against his chest. 'Present for you,' she told him sweetly.

Still squatting there, she watched his lean, hard and hand-some face as he stared down at the furry rabbit. A tingling sensation caught hold of her solar plexus as she watched the tension relax from his lips so they could shift into a reluctant smile, and at last he looked at her. What she saw glinting in his eyes made her so glad she'd taken the flippancy route.

'I thought you'd done another runner,' he admitted.

It took Lexi a second or two to work out why he'd said *another* runner—until she remembered how she'd run back to England three years ago. No note, not even a spitting I hate you note. She'd just walked out of this very hospital, climbed into a taxi, and left.

'Nope.' Still she kept it light. 'I went shopping.' She waved a hand at the rabbit. 'Well, at least say hello to him.'

Silently he passed her back the shoes, then picked the rabbit off his chest and looked at it. 'He's wearing a pink bow round his neck.'

'They didn't have a blue one.'

'Does he have a name?'

'Yes. William,' she announced decisively. 'William Wabbit—because the young man that served me couldn't sound his "r" and his wabbit sounded kind of cute.'

'Rabbit in Italian is *coniglio*.'

'Ah, yes, but the guy was trying out his best English to impress me,' Lexi explained.

'Flirting with you?'

'Of course.' She put the shoes back in the bag. 'He was Italian.'

Instead of plucking all her other purchases off his lap, Franco caught hold of her hand. Even as she glanced up and saw the darkening look in his eyes she sort of knew what was coming next and tried to pull against it. But by then he'd already set her moving forward, her soft gasp the barest protest before her lips made contact with his. Warmth flooded her senses, and the feel of their mouths fused together was so natural already that she almost sank more deeply into the kiss—until she realised what she was doing and pulled back.

'*Grazie,*' he husked. 'For the wabbit.'

Dragging her gaze down to where the rabbit rested against his chest, she murmured, 'You're welcome,' a bit too huskily for her liking, and quickly returned her attention to jumbling her purchases back into the bags.

'How did you know what time I left the hotel?' she asked curiously, fighting to keep her tone light.

This kissing thing had to stop, she was telling herself. OK, so she'd started it. And the kiss just now had only been a typical Italian thank you kiss... But it still had to stop.

She was unaware that Franco was watching her narrowly.

'Pietro arrived to collect you five minutes after you left.'

It was only when he picked it up that she saw his Blackberry had been lying next to the laptop. He handed it to her. 'Put your number in it.'

'So you can keep tabs on me?'

'It's a communication tool not a tracker.'

Pulling a face, she took the phone from him and did as he asked without further comment. While spending the last three hours shopping, she had also been contemplating the current situation she had committed herself to with Franco, and decided that, his having lost the closest friend a man could ever have, she would try her best to fill a small part of the gap Marco had left in Franco's life until he was ready to face up to his loss.

A friend—but not a kissing friend, she determined with a frown as she handed the phone back, aware that her lips still wore the warm impression of his against them.

As he took back the phone, Franco wished he knew what was going on inside her head. Her frown was pensive, the complacent way she had been treating him told him she'd come to some decisions over the night about how she was going to treat being back in his life. The rabbit spoke volumes. The summer they were together she used to produce all kinds of cheap and wacky gifts for him, like the tiny plastic camel on a plinth that gyrated when you pressed the bottom, which she'd insisted looked just like him when he danced. And the set of three little yellow ducks she'd dropped into his bathwater then laughed herself double when they started paddling towards a certain part of his body with a speed that made him stand up fast. Then there was the whole row of frogs in all different sizes and materials, she'd lined up on the shelf above their bed and insisted on kissing each one every night because, she told him, she was convinced at least one of them was going to turn into her handsome Prince.

He had never met anyone like her. She'd been part child and part extraordinarily passionate and deeply sensual woman. And she'd trusted him so totally she did not hold anything back. She'd pinched his clothes, used his toothbrush, and thrown his friends off the *Miranda* when she'd had enough of their company without bothering to ask him if it was OK. If they went out clubbing she would ignore him to dance the night away in the middle of the heaving crush of bodies, laughing, flirting, completely uninhibited, but when she tired of dancing she would locate him like a homing pigeon and drag him away from whatever he was doing, whoever he was with, without apology or even a scant goodnight.

It had never occurred to her that he might tire of her. She'd refused to listen to sly comments about his staying power in a relationship. She'd simply loved him, and believed without question that he was in love with her, so when it had all gone sour she'd been left floundering in a sea of hurt disillusionment that had turned so cold and bitter she'd become a tragically lost stranger to him almost overnight.

He picked up the rabbit and looked at it, grimacing, because he did not doubt that this was Lexi's way of turning back the clock—but only in as far as she was attempting to ease his pain over Marco by reminding him of the time they had spent together without Marco around, he discerned. That kiss, that brief coming together of their mouths, was still burning on his lips; but all he'd seen on Lexi's lips was their faint downturn, and her face showed withdrawal—as if she'd been embarrassed but was valiantly determined to keep the atmosphere light.

Not so for last night's kiss, though, Franco reminded himself grimly. Last night's kiss had been the other Lexi bursting out from behind this one—urgent, passionate and compassionate. *That* was the woman he was determined to get back again.

Glancing up from the rabbit when she stood with her bags and moved over to his bed, he watched as she proceeded to tip everything back out again so she could refold them. Franco slid his eyes down the length of her slender legs and wondered why he'd complained about what she was wearing when the moulding of the black leggings sparked a groin heating flashback to how it felt when those long slender legs were wrapped tightly around his waist. The striped top hugged her slender curves, and she'd tied back her hair this morning, twisting its shiny length into a casual knot that rested low, just above her creamy nape. It would take him one second flat to loosen that hair again, bring it floating down through his waiting fingers. Give him another few seconds and he would—

A phone started ringing. He glanced down at his phone,

only realising it wasn't ringing when Lexi made a dive across his bed to grab her handbag. Plucking out her mobile, she frowned down at the screen for a couple of seconds. He watched her lips crush into a brooding pout.

'Sorry, but I have to take this,' she mumbled, and walked quickly out of the room.

Franco heard her murmur, 'Hi, Bruce,' as the door swung shut behind her, and just like that his mellowing mood turned stark.

Rolling the table away from his legs, he let the steely grip of cold hard anger give him the strength to rise to his feet, wincing when everything hurt, then cursing because it did. Outside the window Livorno was shimmering in the noonday heat. Below him he could see his father's black limo standing in the car park, with Pietro leaning against the bonnet chatting to one of the security men his father had put in place to keep out the intrusive press. Beyond the hospital perimeter he could see a small clutch of camera toting paparazzi, loitering like lazy lizards by the gates. Lexi hadn't mentioned them. He wondered if she'd been hassled by them when she'd arrived today. He knew they were curious—the internet was full of stories about the crash and Marco's tragic death. They'd gone hunting for older stories and dragged out his and Lexi's hasty marriage and even hastier break-up.

There had even been a comment from Bruce Dayton and a photo of him, looking smooth and slick as always, standing outside his agency. 'Lexi Hamilton is naturally devastated by Marco Clemente's death. Of course she is supporting her husband at this tragic time. That is all I am going to say.'

There was no quote from Lexi knocking about on the internet. She had not felt compelled to speak to the press. When Dayton had done so he'd made sure he was standing beside the name of his agency. Nothing like a bit of free publicity if you could get it, the calculating bastard.

And her last name was Tolle—no matter how much Dayton

ignored that fact. Why was he calling her? Did he fear he was about to lose control of her once again? Bruce Dayton was a dangerous control freak where Lexi was concerned. His silvery eyes had used to glint with possessiveness every time he looked at her. When she'd run away from here she'd gone directly to Dayton, who must have been celebrating beneath the caring concern he would have shown her. That Dayton had managed to achieve his goal and get her into his bed with him burned like poison in Franco's blood. Were they still lovers? Was Dayton laying on the pressure right now to bring Lexi back to heel?

Franco picked up his mobile. From the window he watched Pietro accepting his call. Five minutes later he was limping painfully over to the clothes closet and opening the door.

Lexi, meanwhile, was pacing the quiet corridor well away from listening ears. 'Please, listen to me, Bruce—'

'You don't plan to come back here to work, do you?' he challenged harshly.

Lexi winced at his icily accusing tone. 'I haven't said that,' she denied. 'But I do think it's time that you and I took a step back from each other,' she admitted, as gently as she could. 'You said yourself that I need to take a good look at where my life is heading.'

'Right now Lexi, I can see you heading for another big fall.'

'You and I…we were becoming too close for the wrong reasons.'

'Explain that,' Bruce clipped out. 'Are you saying you don't feel anything for me?'

'I care for you deeply, but—'

'You're still in love with that Italian swine,' he said. 'Has it occurred to you that he's plucking on your heartstrings because he's ill and probably looks endearingly pathetic?'

'This conversation has nothing to do with Franco,' she contended.

'Of *course* it's about Franco,' Bruce sliced back. 'He crooks his finger and you go running—'

'No, this is about you opening my eyes to the kind of relationship that has been developing between *us*, and I think I've always known deep down that it's not going to work.' Lexi pressed home, even though she knew it was going to hurt. 'You recognised that too, Bruce,' she reminded him gently. 'I saw it in your expression and heard it in your voice. You've been the most wonderful friend to me—the very best. But somewhere along the line our feelings for each other became confused.'

'Thanks, Lexi, for telling me that you think I'm such a limp-brained fool.'

She gripped the phone more tightly. 'I didn't mean that—'

'Good. Because I am not the one who's confused about my feelings. I can accept that you might need more time to make up your mind about us, but what I can't take is you doing it while hanging around *him*. He's like poison to you, Lexi. He always was and always will be. I will give you until after Clemente's funeral, then you had better be back here pronto or I'm coming to get you—because I am not giving up on us!'

He cut her off. Lexi leant back against the wall and closed her eyes. She should have dealt with this. She should have dealt with it months ago. Now she felt he had every right to be angry with her. The problem was she didn't like hurting people. She knew what it felt like, having been so badly hurt herself. And the worst part was Bruce was not her enemy. Franco was her enemy. If only because of the way he could still make her feel.

Re-entering Franco's room, she found he wasn't there. A glance at the closed bathroom door and she pulled in a deep breath and went back to sorting out the things she'd piled on his bed, glad of the few minutes' respite while she tried to put her conversation with Bruce to one side.

The door to the bathroom opened. Turning around, Lexi almost dropped down onto the bed when a fully dressed Franco stepped out—a Franco she never had grown used to seeing like this. It felt as if someone had stuck a live wire in between her ribs, and the electric sensation tingled all the way down to her toes.

He was wearing a dark pinstriped suit of such amazing quality it seemed to glide over his long, lean physique like a living, moving thing.

'You can't get dressed,' she breathed out in trembling objection. 'Why have you got dressed?'

Managing to drag her gaze away from its mesmerised stare at the neat red tie knotted against the pristine white shirt collar that showed off the deep golden skin beneath his chin, she felt it clash with a set of rock-hard handsome features that bore little resemblance to the man she'd been looking at ten minutes before—the man she remembered as the Franco she'd used to know.

Not this one, though. This one was the married version— the one she'd learnt was a horribly cold, distant stranger who could look at her through the impassive dark eyes of a ruthless decision maker, as he was doing right now. She wrapped her arms around herself, shivering in response to the look.

'We are leaving,' he said. No embroidery to that declaration. He simply stepped over to the table with barely a limp on show and closed down his laptop, then picked up his phone.

'I—I don't understand.' Flicking a glance at the bell push dangling over the pillows on the bed, she wondered anxiously if this was another one of his agitated moments and if she needed to bring someone in here fast, before he did himself some damage.

'It is pretty simple. I have been unplugged, I am off all medication, and now I want to get away from this place.'

'You mean they've signed you off?'

Glittering eyes set between narrowed eyelashes sent her a grimly mocking look. 'Who are *they*, precisely?'

'The...' She waved a hand. 'The doctors and—whoever. You can't just walk out because you feel like it, Franco. There might be something really wrong with—'

'You did.'

Cut off midsentence, Lexi blinked at him. 'Excuse me?' she breathed.

'You walked out of here without being "signed off," as you descriptively put it.' Putting the phone in his pocket, he gathered up the fluffy rabbit next and carried it over to where she stood by the bed. 'Actually, you ran.'

Having glued her attention to his legs, looking for a pronounced limp or something to indicate whether it hurt him to walk, Lexi jerked up her head. As if her surprised little world had just gone topsy-turvy, she found herself having to look up—and up—to reach the hard contours of his face. A clattering mass reaction stopped her breathing. It was so long since they'd stood toe to toe like this. Seeing him lying in bed or even sitting in a chair had *not* jolted her memory banks into reminding her of just how tall Franco was.

And it wasn't just the extra inches of height he had over her—it was the sheer breadth of him and the illicit vibration of dangerously exciting power idling beneath the suit. He towered over her and her mouth dried up. She blinked and was suddenly assailed with an image of him, all golden tan and ridged muscles, standing over her just like this, wearing only a pair of white boxer shorts. A shockingly terrible tingle attacked the tips of her breasts, then shot like a flaming arrow to the vulnerable place between her legs. Liquid heat poured into the same place, making her squeeze in a sharp, choky little breath, and her skin broke out in a hot-cold sweat.

'And I'm not even touching you,' Franco chided softly, reading the choky gasp because he remembered it so well. *'Yet,'* he added with silken purpose, just to see what would happen to her next.

A tide of interesting colour washed up her slender white

throat and the black of her pupils dilated until they'd almost completely obliterated the ocean-blue of her irises.

'This potent effect we have on each other is one hell of an aphrodisiac, *cara*,' he murmured delicately. 'Do you want to know what you are doing to me?'

Lexi slowly lowered her eyes in an effort to break free from his scintillating spell. She felt dizzy, and tiny muscles all over her were contracting so tightly they pulsed.

'Y-you have no reason to run.' Valiantly, she locked the single brain cell she seemed to have left on what he'd said before.

'But you did?'

Pinning her lips together, and realising that they felt plumped up and tingly, Lexi nodded her head, finding she had to part her lips again so that she could speak. 'And I will do it again if you don't turn off the sexual pressure.'

His mouth broke into a wolfishly amused grin. 'Good to know I've still got it, *amore*.'

'You and how many others?' Lexi derided his insufferable self-belief, at the same time deriding all the other good-looking men with truckloads of sexual charisma she met on a day-to-day basis—not one of whom came anywhere near making her feel what Franco made her feel.

That he'd completely misunderstood her meaning hit her as she watched his eyes cool. Even his cheeks suddenly looked carved, as if someone had scooped any hint of softness out of them. Lexi felt the sudden need to redistribute her weight equally between her two booted feet, and she unfolded her arms to drop them down to her sides, her fingers curling into fists.

'You mis—'

'Spare me the numbers.'

Turning abruptly away from her, he pushed the stuffed rabbit into one of her bags. The moment she lost his attention Lexi reached out and snatched up the bell press; gave it a long and urgent push. He caught the movement and swung back. Lexi dropped the bell push as if it was hot. As his eyes narrowed on her like stinging lasers she pushed her chin up and fed him back a wide-eyed look of sparking defiance.

To her total astonishment Franco threw back his dark head and laughed. 'So even you think I've gone crazy!'

There was no 'even you' about it. Lexi had considered him crazy ever since she'd arrived here. He might be reading her every thought and feeling, but she found she couldn't keep up with his thought patterns or the fast changes in his mood.

'You're not leaving here without someone's say-so.' She struck a stubborn pose.

'Pietro will be here in five minutes,' was all he commented, as if that was enough to relay his intentions. 'I sent him to your hotel to settle the bill and collect your things.'

The door swung open before Lexi could respond to that piece of smooth forward planning. Dr Cavelli walked in, then stopped when he saw his patient was dressed and standing.

As cool and casual as a long drink of water, Franco turned and strode across the room, a smile on his face and his hand outstretched. 'Thank you,' he murmured in smooth as balm Italian, 'for the wonderful care and attention I have received from you and your staff. However, it is time for me leave.'

The doctor had been staring at the limp free way Franco had been moving, but he jerked his eyes up to the outstretched hand, then even further, staring dubiously at Franco's beautifully polite mask of a face. 'I am not sure…'

'I am drug free and feeling much better,' Franco pointed out in a dulcet tone, then waited as if he had the patience of a saint while the doctor glanced questioningly at Lexi and she sent a helplessly bewildered shrug in return.

'There is no medical reason why you cannot be discharged, *signor*,' Dr Cavelli murmured cautiously. 'However, you will need to keep a watchful eye on your bruising for the next week or two. The risk of blood clots has not diminished, and you will need the dressings changed on your thigh wound.'

'Alexia and I will promise to keep a watchful eye out for blood clots,' Franco assured him, refusing to look at Lexi even though he was holding his breath in case she told him she was not prepared to do anything of the kind. 'And I am capable of changing my own dressings.'

The doctor looked at Lexi again as though he was waiting for her to confirm that she would be there to take care of his patient. Parting her lips with the intention of refusing to have any part in Franco's plans to walk out of there, she happened to glance at him—saw the evidence of strain showing in his proud profile and the grim tension in his elegant stance. She remembered Marco, experienced a swooping sensation deep down inside that felt as if something was twisting her organs together painfully, and she closed her mouth again, then gave a silent nod of her head.

The tension holding Franco together sprang free, almost toppling him from his increasingly painful stance. Whatever Dayton had said to her on the phone, he had not yanked on her chains hard enough—but Franco had. Sheer grim satisfaction helped to keep him upright through the ordeal of receiving the doctor's detailed advice on maintaining his present rate of recovery. By then Pietro had arrived and, ignoring the older man's shocked consternation when he realised what was going on, Franco quietly instructed him to collect his bag from the adjoining bathroom.

He almost collapsed into the rear of his father's limo. He was that exhausted by keeping up the appearance that he was magically returned to robust health.

Lexi sat beside him, flitting from concern to annoyance and back again as she studied the way he was sitting there, deathly pale with his eyes closed, one long-fingered hand pressed against his chest inside his jacket, the other lying limp on the seat between them. She could see the punch holes from the shunt on the back of his hand and the bruising circling them. But what really bothered her was the shallowness of his breathing.

'It would serve you right if you had a relapse now, Franco, what with your wicked, lying stupidity!' she launched at him, anxiety feeding her hot temper.

'I left that particularly drastic kind of wicked, lying stupidity to Marco,' Franco relayed flatly in response.

# CHAPTER FIVE

LEXI swivelled around to stare at him. 'M-Marco?' she prompted, watching warily for a sign of that awful grey pallor to sink down across Franco's face. The trouble was that he was already that greyish colour.

'Pietro, the paparazzi—are they following us?'

He did it yet again. Blocked out the subject of his best friend.

'*Si,*' the older man responded. 'They sit on our tail like reckless fools. You want me to lose them?'

'You think that you can do it?'

'Ah, *si*, of course I can do it.'

'What paparazzi?' As Lexi twisted around to take a look through the back window an eager Pietro threw the car into an acute left turn.

Trying not to wince as the swerving action lanced through him like a knife, Franco told her dryly, 'They have been on your tail since you arrived in Livorno.'

'Oh.' She twisted back in her seat. 'I've stopped bothering to look for them since I gave up acting.'

'Why did you give up acting?' Turning his head against the seat-back, he looked at her. 'You were supposed to have a glittering Hollywood career waiting for you when you left me.'

Ignoring his last remark, even though he'd made it sound

as if she'd walked away from him because of her glittering career prospects, Lexi said with a shrug, 'Acting was never my dream. It was my mother's dream.' Poor Grace, who'd so wanted to be a famous Hollywood movie star all her life. 'I fell into the movie thing by accident when I was fooling around with a script off set during one of my mother's auditions. Someone heard me, dragged me onto the set, then made me read the same bit again. I did. I got the part.' As she looked at Franco she caught a faintly unsettling glint in his narrowed eyes.

'You never told me that before.'

'You probably never asked before. Why the sinister glint?' she demanded suspiciously.

'It is not sinister. So, what was *your* dream?'

Looking foreward again, Lexi didn't answer him. Her dream had been way too basic for a man like Franco to understand. A house with a garden, lots of kids, and a husband who worked a nine-to-five job then came home to his family each evening.

Growing up in a city apartment with a single mum who'd worked the oddest hours possible meant that she'd more or less brought herself up. Her garden—her playground—had been the set of one small movie or another, or the cloistered walls of her mother's dressing room backstage.

No, her childhood dreams had found no romance in the acting world.

'*My* mother dreamed of me becoming a great concert pianist,' he said, lifting up his hands and spreading out his long fingers to study them with a rueful grimace. 'All I wanted to do was to mess around with boats and engines.'

But he still played the piano like nobody else Lexi had ever heard. He could bring the whole of Monfalcone to a breathless listening standstill with a hauntingly beautiful piece of classical music played on the grand piano in the main salon, or he could ratchet up a flagging party by belting out a wild medley of pop, hot jazz and heavy rock.

With those same long blunt fingers that took apart a boat engine with such dedicated care and knowledge.

'She was beautiful—your mother,' Lexi murmured, recalling the painting that hung in the same salon that contained the grand piano.

'As was yours.' Lowering his hands, he looked at her and an ache that came very close to mutual understanding tugged like a gentle weight on her heart. 'I'm sorry I never got to meet her.'

So was Lexi. Grace would have fallen in love with Franco—the tall, dark Italian with oodles of bone-melting charm. She didn't think that his mother would have fallen in love with her, though. Isabella Tolle had been hewn from a different breed entirely from Lexi—and Grace, come to that. Grace had been an eternal dreamer, whereas Isabella Tolle had been born with all of her dreams already mapped out and secured for her.

And the last thing she would have wanted for her only son would have been a hasty marriage to a one-hit movie star who'd set out to trap him... No. Lexi stopped that thought in its tracks. She had not *set out* to trap him. She just *had* trapped him, and learned to hate herself for doing it.

'Do we go to the apartment or Monfalcone?'

Franco's casual question intruded, making Lexi blink a couple of times before she could focus her attention back on him. Remembering what his father had said to her that morning, she said, 'Monfalcone,' though with the thoughts now rattling around in her head—all to do with her time spent living there—she wished she hadn't agreed to that part of her bargain with Salvatore.

'We go home, Pietro,' he relayed to the driver.

'Ah, *si, si.*' Pietro smiled in approval. 'That is good *signor.* That is very good indeed...'

'At least one person approves of us, *bella mia*,' Franco drawled softly.

Lexi shifted restlessly on the seat. She wasn't sure that she liked the lazily veiled look Franco was levelling at her from his corner of the car. It made the hairs on the back of her neck tingle as if she was missing something important here that she should be working out.

'We are not an "us."' It needed saying—just in case Franco was having amorous ideas about the two of them.

'What are we, then?'

She opened her mouth to answer, then closed it again. She did not have an answer to what they were. Estranged husband and wife? A bit more than that, since she was returning to Monfalcone with him like a wife. Friends, then? No. Once upon a time Franco had been the closest thing to a friend she'd ever known—until she'd discovered he was only in the relationship for the fun of the sex, and of course, the bet. The only other reason had to be Marco. She was here with him because he'd lost his closest friend. But she was not allowed to mention that.

Frowning, she shook her head and turned her face to the window, leaving the question to hang in the air. Franco studied her taut profile and felt an ache deep down inside, like a battering ram trying to bridge the gap between them so he could answer the question for her the physical way.

Great strategy, Francesco, he mocked himself grimly. The doctors had gagged her, he had chained her to his side, and his father had used subtle manipulation to bring Lexi back to Monfalcone with Franco. Now you want to ruin it all with a smash-and-grab approach you are not physically capable of carrying out.

And then there was that other unknown element stirring around in the soup of their fragile relationship. 'What did Dayton call to say to you?' he prompted coolly.

The way he'd used Bruce's last name spoke volumes to

Lexi. Franco had always disliked Bruce as much as Bruce disliked him. 'I work for him.'

'I know you do.'

He did? That surprised her. She'd thought he'd shut her right out of his life, much as he was doing with Marco right now. Another bad thing obliterated from Franco's world.

'Well, then—you are an employer, so you know how it works. Don't ask stupid questions.' Lexi reacted stiffly, turning away again. She refused to discuss Bruce with him, because... Well, because she was loyal to the people that she loved, and right now she loved Bruce more than she loved...

Back-pedalling desperately, determined not to face what she had been about to think, Lexi moved in the seat as if she was trying to push something truly frightening away from her. And maybe she was, she admitted, aware of why she had severed that last too disturbing thought before it could round itself off.

I don't even have the excuse of a tragic accident to make me block out that which I don't want to face, she recognised grimly.

The journey continued with silence thickening the car's confines. The silent smoothness of the drive was a testament to the quality of luxury engineering and design.

Lexi slowly sank back in her seat and watched the view pass by them beyond the glass, tinted against the fierce rays of the sun. This part of Italy had to be one of the most beautiful places on earth, she observed hazily. The afternoon sunlight coloured everything such a warm golden colour, and the sheer stately elegance of tall tapering cypress trees dotted miles and miles of undulating landscape. Even the occasional silvery spread of an ancient olive tree rising up on its sturdy twisting trunk made an impact, as if one of the great Italian masters had placed them there with the gifted touch of his paintbrush. Familiar scents teased her nostrils and heightened her senses. Warm like the place, sweet and exotic.

Turning to look at Franco, she discovered that he'd fallen asleep. An achy little pang twisted inside her: even in sleep he did not look comfortable. Tension clung to the perfect symmetry of his face, pulling his sensual mouth down at the corners. He had slipped his hand back inside his jacket to cover the area around his cracked ribs, while the other hand seemed be lightly gripping his injured thigh. Perhaps they should have gone to his apartment and not added the extra half-hour drive to Monfalcone, she considered worriedly. Perhaps she should have put up a much fiercer fight against his leaving the hospital in the first place.

'Not much longer now, *signora*.'

The quietness of Pietro's voice brought Lexi's anxious gaze into contact with the driver's mirror, where Pietro's dark eyes reflected the same concern that she was feeling over Franco, for he had noticed his discomfort too.

She sent Pietro a small nod to acknowledge his reassurance. 'The press?' she whispered.

'They gave up once they realised where we are going.'

To a house surrounded by acres of private land they would not dare to encroach upon, Lexi thought as she slid her gaze back to the window. Another mile or so and they would turn off the main highway to head towards the hill she could see rising up in the near distance. Once over the crest of that hill they would drop into a spectacularly beautiful valley, with rolling pastures and meadows gently dipping down towards the river that meandered its way the length of the valley on its way to the sea. Once they had crossed the ancient narrow stone bridge that forged the river they would be on Monfalcone land.

Great, she thought as they crested the hill, and unhappy memories began to surface of the long, lonely weeks she'd spent trying to make herself as invisible as possible in this breathtakingly beautiful but inhospitable place. She'd been her own worst enemy—so totally off the scale of hormonal upheaval that even small problems became huge mountainous things she just didn't know how to deal with.

As if by sheer homing instinct Franco stirred and opened his eyes as they slowed down to negotiate the narrow bridge over the river. Lexi saw him wince as he tried to change the position he'd been sleeping in.

'All right?' she questioned huskily.

'*Si,*' he said, but he wasn't, and the brief, tense, wry smile he turned on her pricked at that ache she'd been feeling. It was not going to go away any time soon.

From the bridge they drove onto a long and narrow undulating ribbon of tarmac flanked by two rows of elegant cypress trees that made a grand statement about the house they were heading towards even before it came into view. As the car sped them down the lane the sunlight blinked in and out between each evenly spaced tree trunk with perfect regularity. Lexi knew from experience the effect could be dangerously hypnotic if you didn't concentrate all your attention on the road ahead.

She knew because she'd fallen prey to it once, driving away from the house in floods of tears that had only helped to amplify the phenomenon, and she'd ended up crashing the car into one of the shallow drain ditches situated on the other side of the trees. How she'd missed making solid impact with a tree she would never know. She'd just been lucky, she supposed. Not that Francesco had seen her relatively soft landing nose-down in the ditch as fortunate. He'd been furious. He'd called her 'bloody reckless and stupid' as he'd hauled her body out of the crunched car in a rage.

'Were you hoping to kill yourself, or just the baby?'

Lexi shivered as the angry echo of his voice broke over her. She'd sobbed her heart out right there in the middle of the road, and he'd taken her in his arms and let her cry herself silent. As silent as Franco had been throughout the whole wretched weeping jag, while her little car had shone silver in the ditch and his flashy red one had simmered a couple of yards away, with its driver's door hanging open and the engine still running.

'I did not know what to say to you.'

The quietly deep, slightly constrained timbre of his voice brought her eyes round to look at him. He was staring out of the other window, but as she turned her head so did he, and she was snared in the sombre darkness of his eyes. Through the flickering play of sunlight across his face Lexi saw the bleakness of the same painful recollection.

'I was out of control.' She made the confession with husky thickness, because it was the first time she'd ever accepted that. 'I set out to make your life miserable and I succeeded.'

'You say that as if I behaved like a saint.' A grim smile clipped the corners of his mouth. 'You had too much to deal with at one time. You were carrying our baby. You had just lost your mother...'

And she'd known deep down that she should have lost him too, but she'd hung onto him—clung to him even while she'd hated him by then. Staring down at her hands where they lay pleated together on her lap, Lexi felt a tremor cross her lips. Yes, she'd been out of control, both emotionally and hormonally, long before she'd crashed her car into that ditch.

They'd come here from England after burying her mother. Franco had seen to everything, even though Bruce had insisted that *he* should do it. It was into the middle of that angry argument between the two men that she'd dropped the news that she was pregnant. Bruce had reacted by thumping Franco. Strangely, Franco had taken the punch without retaliating at all. He'd been too stunned by her announcement, she'd realised later, but at the time...

'I took the high-handed noble route and rushed you into marriage when what you really needed to do was to curl up somewhere on your own and grieve for your *mamma*...'

Poor Grace, who'd spent her life dreaming of fame, but whose death had made barely a ripple on the surface of the news media—while her daughter's hasty marriage to Francesco Tolle had earned headlines across two countries. He was right. She had been given no time to grieve before she'd been plunged into wedding arrangements right here at Monfalcone. No one here had met or even heard of Grace Hamilton. They had been strangers to Lexi—coldly polite strangers who disapproved of her because they believed she'd ruined Franco's life. They'd grieved for *him* while she'd just felt isolated, caged in by her own private grief she did not feel she could express. And the worst thing of all was that she'd known Franco had already started to cool their relationship before all the rest had happened.

San Remo... The place that had brought an end to their summer madness and begun their long winter of hell.

The car slowed down again, the cypress trees having given way to a high, neatly clipped box hedge that helped to hide the house from view. Two intricately designed iron gates bearing the Monfalcone crest in gold swung open in a gap in the hedge as they approached, and from there the full glory of a classical Italian garden opened up in front of them like some breath-takingly beautiful film set, complete with dancing fountains and lichen-stained statues surrounded by strictly regimented pathways edged by more low, clipped box hedge.

In the background stood Monfalcone, its deep gold stone walls basking in the afternoon sun. Once upon a time there had been a moat, complete with drawbridge to pull up across the coach entrance that led into the inner courtyard when feuding neighbours came to call. The moat had been filled in long ago. Now neat lawns formed a skirt around the outer walls, and the drawbridge had been replaced by another set of iron gates that Lexi had never seen closed.

As they plunged into the ink darkness of the deep stone

arch the sultry warm air developed such a distinct chill that
Lexi shivered and goosebumps rose on her flesh. Then they
were out again, and driving into a huge sunny courtyard
where deep, gracefully arching upper and lower terraces
flanked each wing of the house. When she'd first come here
Lexi had been in awe of the sheer classical splendour of her
surroundings. The interior was just as elegant as the exte-
rior—a place of pale cool marble and richly polished wood
and the kind of furniture collected through many centuries
that somehow lived comfortably side by side.

On one level she'd loved this place for its surprisingly
warm and relaxed form of living. On another level she'd hated
it because she'd been so unhappy here. She wasn't sure how
she was going to feel this time around—it probably depended
on the memories evoked by coming back here.

Franco obviously did not have the same uncertainty, for
he opened his door the moment the car came to a stop at the
front entrance. The long hiss he made at his first attempt to
get out of the car dragged Lexi's attention to him. As she'd
feared, his bruised body had stiffened up during the journey,
making it painful for him to move.

'Wait, I'll come round and help you,' she said quickly, and
scrambled out of the car as Pietro did the same thing.

Gravel crunched beneath the soles of her boots as she shot
around the back of the limo, only to find that Franco had already hauled himself upright and was standing in a ray of
sunlight, his face turned up to it as if he was paying homage
to its golden warmth.

Lexi pulled to a jerky standstill, her breath trapped in her
throat. He looked so much taller and younger, strikingly handsome, and yet so very vulnerable standing there like that. She
knew instinctively what he was doing. Not once in the last
twenty-four hours had it occurred to her that he might have
believed he would not live to see his home again, that com-

ing back here had been the powerful force driving him today. Suddenly all the strange things Franco had been meting out since his accident were afforded a painful kind of sense in this moment of silent homage.

Then the two long glass-fronted doors swept open and Zeta appeared—a short round woman with silver hair swept back from her plump, anxious face. Her eyes barely grazed across Lexi before they swept to Franco.

'Just look at you,' she scolded him. 'You are not fit to be walking, never mind leaving the safety of the hospital. Are you crazy or something?'

'*Buongiorno*, Zeta,' Franco responded dryly. 'It is good to see you too.'

Zeta huffed out a breath, then threw up her hands as if in despair. 'If your *papà* had any wits left after you robbed him of them he would—'

'Do you think I could cross the threshold into my home before I am henpecked?' Franco cut in.

Quivering with wounded pride and emotion, the house-keeper stepped to one side of the doorway. Both Lexi and Pietro leapt to offer Franco support.

'I can do this by myself,' he ground out, making them all freeze, including Zeta, and watch as he pushed his long body into movement and managed to walk past the housekeeper without revealing so much as a hint of pain.

Once he'd made it into the house all three rushed to stand in the doorway, tense, like three runners standing on the starting line, ready to move with the sound of the gun.

Lexi wanted to yell at him that displays of macho pride and stubbornness did nothing for her! But he was already negotiating the stairs by then, and she swallowed the words whole in case she encouraged him to make a sudden movement that would cause him to lose his balance.

He did it. Mr Macho and Stubborn made it all the way up

those polished wood stairs to the galleried landing above. The moment he was safely there, Lexi released her pent-up tension with, 'I hope you feel very pleased with yourself for achieving that—because I don't!'

He turned his head to look down on her. 'Very pleased,' he admitted, and then one of his really charismatic rakish smiles appeared, to soften the strain from his features. 'Now you can come up and help me out of this uncomfortable suit.'

Arrogant too, she thought, and responded accordingly. She tossed up her chin and turned to Pietro. 'Either you go up there and help him, or I go up there and kill him,' she said, her eyes alight with simmering defiance.

Too late, she sensed Zeta's shock. Too late, she regretted her impulsive reaction. For the housekeeper was now recalling months of spitting rows and seething atmospheres.

Pietro just pressed a reassuring kiss to his wife's cheek, then bent to collect their bags, which he'd dropped to the floor ready to race to Franco's rescue if he'd started to sway.

'I will put your bags in your old room, *signora*,' he told Lexi, and headed off up the stairs.

Leaving Lexi facing a definitely disapproving house-keeper.

She could see that Zeta was envisaging a return to the hostilities of three years ago. Back then Lexi would have an-swered her look with burning defiance. This time she heaved out a wavering sigh instead. 'He knew he was pushing his luck too far when he said that,' she said in defence of her sharpness. 'And he frightened me… Hello, Zeta,' she con-cluded, and stuck out her hand in the hope that the Tolles' loyal housekeeper would see it as a proffered olive branch meant to try and put their past tense relationship aside.

After a few seconds of silent study Zeta nodded her head and took Lexi's hand. They were not quite up to hugging and kissing each other, but at least it was a start.

A start for what? The question pulled Lexi's breath up

short. She just had to work out what she was doing here, be-cause—well, because it was beginning to feel permanent, and that was dangerous…

'What is she doing?' Franco asked as Pietro helped him out of his jacket.

'I believe I heard her threatening to kill you,' the older man responded evenly, and was rewarded with a crooked half smile, which quickly disappeared into a frown.

'We make her welcome here this time, Pietro,' he in-structed grimly. 'It is important to me.'

'I know, sir.' Laying the jacket aside, Pietro turned to help Franco unbutton his shirt, but his hands were impatiently waved away.

Franco was aching all over, and all he wanted to do was fall onto his bed. Even heeling off his shoes was agony, and he wondered how the hell he'd managed to put the shoes on in the first place.

Bloody-minded willpower and a grim determination to be in control of what was happening around him and to him.

'I will do the rest.' He turned away from Pietro's hovering need to help. 'Find out if my wife—'

*My wife*… The possessive title sounded so alien on his tongue it stopped his thoughts stone dead. He had rarely called Lexi that even when they were together—he'd rarely thought about her in those terms.

Then he remembered the last time he'd used the posses-sive term—to Marco—and experienced a different type of pain.

'Check if she has eaten lunch today,' he said, frowning again. He knew he'd deliberately missed out the *my wife* part because he did not feel he had the right to use it—not yet, anyway.

'Have *you* eaten?' Pietro was still hovering like a man who needed to do something helpful, but all Franco could think of was lying down on that bed.

*'Si,'* he said, though it was not the truth—but it saved him having to deal with further questions over choices of food. Or—worse—Zeta turning her kitchen upside down and making him his all his favourite foods to tempt his appetite, like she'd used to do when he was a boy and sick with some childhood ailment. 'If you would tell Lexi—' No. He changed that, smiling crookedly again. 'If you would *ask* Lexi to come and see me after she has settled in?'

A silent nod and Pietro reluctantly departed. The moment the door closed behind him Franco gave up trying to remove his shirt and just rolled down carefully onto the bed. He would lie there for a couple of minutes to get his breath back, then…

The lingering effects of the drugs still moving around his system and exhaustion from the journey claimed him like a heavy blanket, and Franco knew nothing else.

He certainly did not know that Lexi had taken time for a shower and to change out of her dark city clothes, which were sticking to her overheated skin, into one of her new dresses that were more in keeping with a late summer in Italy. Then Zeta had arrived with a tray of tea and light pastries, which she'd discovered she was hungry enough to sit down and enjoy.

Over an hour later she let herself out of the suite she had been allocated all those years ago—two whole wings of the house away from Franco's suite. Once deeply intimate lovers turned into married strangers, she mused as she walked the long corridors. What had the separate bedrooms said about their chance of making anything of their fated marriage? About as much chance as they'd both allowed it—which was basically none.

A grimace worked its way across her lips as she arrived at Franco's door. About to lay a soft knock on it, she stalled her knuckles half an inch from their target when she heard a muffled noise that sounded very like a broken sob. A jolt of alarm had her bypassing the polite knock, and she just grabbed the handle and pushed the door open—only to freeze in dismay at the scene that met her unsuspecting gaze.

Franco was sitting on the side of his bed and he was not alone. Claudia Clemente, Marco's beautiful sister, was kneeling at his feet between his spread thighs, her red-tipped fingers clutching at his head while she sobbed into his chest.

Almost anyone else walking in on this moving scene would have felt their heart rend in aching sympathy for both Franco and Claudia, but to Lexi it felt as if someone had reached into her chest and yanked her heart out. She would not have been surprised if she'd turned to stone where she stood. For Claudia was the woman who'd sent proof of that bet to her mobile phone years ago. She was also the woman Franco had spent the night with while Lexi had lost their baby and grieved alone.

# CHAPTER SIX

THROBBING with the need to just turn around, walk out of there and never come back again, Lexi felt nailed to the spot by the rush of emotions that flooded inside her. She was hurting. She was hurting so badly she might as well have been standing there like this three and a half years ago, witnessing their betrayal. They even had a bed there as a gut jerking prop.

A barely controllable desire to go over there and yank the dainty, black clad figure away from Franco and then punch him on his red lipstick stained mouth almost got the better of her. At that precise moment she did not care that Claudia was Marco's kid sister, or that the two of them had every excuse to be indulging in a moment of shared agony.

How had Claudia got in here anyway? Had Zeta let her in? Pietro? One of the maids? Did Claudia have such a free run of this house that she could stroll into Franco's bedroom without needing permission from anyone?

As if she'd been dropped behind a haze of misty red, she watched as Franco glanced up and noticed her standing here.

'Lexi,' he murmured, and sounded so thick and strained that the swinging punch scenario replayed itself in her head. He was either really turned on or close to tears, and the latter she refused to accept—mainly because it just didn't suit the unforgiving frame of mind she was in.

It clearly didn't suit him either, because she saw two streaks of colour shoot high across his cheeks.

Guilty and with an eye witness, she noted.

She hated him.

Claudia lifted her face up off his chest and turned her beautiful dark head. She was two years older than Lexi. Once upon a time those two years had felt more like a decade to Lexi, in smooth sophistication and worldly experience. Now the age-gap felt like nothing at all, and Claudia's amazing sloe-shaped bottomless black eyes were still the most exotically beautiful eyes she had ever seen. She looked nothing like her light-haired, blue-eyed brother. She certainly did not have Marco's sunny temperament. Claudia was devious, calculating and jealously possessive of both her brother and of Franco.

'Lexi,' Marco's beautiful sister whispered as she climbed slowly to her feet. 'I did not expect to see you here.'

Lexi believed it. Claudia was so visibly shocked to see her standing there she could not contain the horror from sounding in her voice.

Lexi did not spare Franco another glance. Her insides had gone into meltdown and were churning up with the ugliest kind of bitterness. It took all of her control to keep breathing in and out. She kept her eyes focused on Claudia, who was wearing the silver wash of tears glistening on the tips of her long black eyelashes.

Crocodile tears? No, that was just too mean for her even to think it.

Claudia had just lost her beloved brother, after all. Of course she would want to come here and commiserate with Franco over their mutual loss. She had the right.

But it was still difficult for Lexi to part her bloodless lips and murmur, 'Hello, Claudia,' peeling her tense fingers off the door handle and still feeling the tension in them when she dropped them to her sides.

*Deep breath, Lexi. Walk forward*, she instructed her legs, which tingled because they did not want her to go anywhere near Claudia Clemente. 'I'm so very sorry about Marco.'

At least that was a genuine response. She offered commiserating kisses to the other woman's cheeks and felt Claudia's floral perfume dry her throat. From the corner of her eye she caught the way Franco's facial muscles clenched when she said Marco's name.

Well, too late for that, she thought, with a cold feeling that sat like a lump where her understanding and sympathy should be. With Claudia here there was no way he could avoid talking about Marco. With Claudia here there was no way he could continue pretending the accident had not happened, or that Lexi was the only person he could bear to have close.

'Oh, please don't say his name,' Claudia begged, and her fabulous eyes filled up with fresh tears. 'I think I am going to die from my grief.'

As a sob broke free from her throat Lexi felt a pang of guilt for suspecting the quality of her grief. Whatever else Claudia was that she despised, she could not take away from her that she'd adored her older brother. Pushing her own stony feelings aside, Lexi plucked a box of tissues from the bedside table and quietly encouraged Claudia to dry her tears.

'I had to come,' Claudia explained once she'd regained control again. 'I knew that Franco would be tormenting himself. I needed to tell him that we do not hold him to blame.'

Well, that was truly thoughtful and caring of her, but while Claudia was busy dabbing her eyes Franco had closed his eyes and was turning that sickly shade of grey.

'And M-Mamma and Papa needed to know if he would be well enough to attend M-Marco's funeral next Tuesday.'

'We will be there.' The man himself spoke at last. Then he fell into deep, dark, husky Italian, spoken too fast for Lexi to follow; but that sent Claudia to her knees again, her arms locking tightly around his neck.

Lexi removed herself over to the window and stayed there until Claudia made her final farewells and eventually left. The ensuing silence hung like a woodchopper's axe, hesitating over the downward slice that would split them clean in two.

Three and a half years was a long time to hang onto such a poisonous grudge, she tried hard to tell herself. She'd grown up an awful lot in those years, so it was logical that Claudia had done the same thing.

Deep down, though, she didn't believe that Marco's sister *had* changed. She'd seen something in the possessive trail of the other woman's fingers as they'd let go of Franco, and in the way she hadn't been able to resist bruising his lips with a final kiss before she'd dragged herself away from him.

The atmosphere she'd left behind pulsated with Lexi's continued silence.

*What am I doing here?*

Once again she asked herself that question. Franco needed people like Claudia around him—friends, family, lovers who would gently ease his grief out into the open.

'What's wrong, Lexi?' he murmured quietly.

'How did she get in here?' she asked.

'She arrived a few minutes ago. I could not deny her need to see me.'

She twisted around to look at him. 'In your bedroom?'

'I was asleep.' Raking slightly unsteady fingers through his hair, he explained, 'Zeta woke me to tell me that Claudia was here. Apparently she had driven here directly from the hospital after discovering I—we had left.'

Lexi nodded her head. It was weird how she was feeling— kind of closed off and iced over. 'You talked with her about Marco?'

Rubbing his hands over his face, Franco nodded. 'What time is it?' He frowned down at his watch. He was still using the same blocking tactics against her where Marco was concerned, Lexi noted. 'I could do with a drink. My mouth is parched. Do you want one?' He was reaching for the house phone beside the bed.

'If you like I can call Claudia back in here and let her share a drink with us,' Lexi suggested coolly.

'What is this?' He frowned. 'So you walked in here and found Claudia in my bedroom? It isn't as if I am in a fit state to seduce the poor woman. You always were a jealous cat about her.'

'Marco said—'

'Marco is not here any longer to say anything!' Driving himself to his feet, he groaned and struggled to gain his balance.

His shirt was hanging open, Lexi saw. His trousers resting low on his waist. He was no longer strapped up there, she noticed, and the extent of his bruising was horribly dark. Unable to stop her eyes from following the shock of dark hair that ran down his front, she imagined a pair of red tipped fingers stroking over him and felt her insides grow hard.

'Marco once warned me that you would probably end up marrying Claudia,' she persisted despite his attempt to head her off. 'He believed the two of you were made for each other—that bringing your two volatile temperaments together would be like capturing forked lightning.'

'Explosive?' Franco said dryly. 'I am not volatile. You are the volatile one in this relationship.'

But they did not have a relationship—that was the whole point! They had a marriage certificate, a load of miserable memories to share, and that was *all* they had!

'I'm going out for a walk.' Lexi made the decision on impulse; but once she had made it she discovered that she couldn't get out of there fast enough.

On a growl of pure frustration, Franco raked out, 'What the hell has got into you?'

Lexi whipped out through the door before he could say

anything else. Inside she was a shaking mess of pain and—oh, God—fear. Fear because she knew she was already emotionally involved again. Attached, attracted, needy and jealous and—

'You go out, *signora*?' One of the maids she remembered from the last time she was here was crossing the hall as Lexi walked quickly towards the rear of the house.

Biting into the inner tissue of her tense lips Lexi nodded her head. 'I need some fresh air,' she mumbled, making a hasty exit.

Once outside, she crossed the terracotta floor of the shady loggia that ran the length of the back of the house, then walked down the steps into the gardens—that spread out in front of her without the rigid formality so carefully nurtured at the front. Several gravel pathways wound their lazy way through informal flowerbeds down towards a small lake she could see glinting a short distance away, beyond the assortment of fruit trees that dappled the paths with leafy shade from the heat of the sun.

She did not know where she was going, though the lake seemed to lure her. Inside she felt as if she'd been switched off like a light.

Upstairs, standing in the window, Franco watched her make her bid for escape with a grating sense of déjà-vu. Cursing softly, because every movement was such damn agony, he looked around for his mobile phone, accessed Lexi's number, and rang it.

She did not have her phone with her, he realised a minute later. Frustration biting at his temper, he walked across the room and headed out onto the landing, then strode the corridors to Lexi's wing of the house. This was something that was about to change around here, he decided grimly as he let himself into her room, then stood for a few seconds, needing to catch his laboured breathing before he went to hunt down her bag and pluck her mobile phone from its capacious depths.

Back in his own room, he used the house phone to relay instructions to Zeta about where his wife would be sleeping tonight, then instructed the housekeeper to send one of the maids to him.

Lexi had located the old wooden bench she'd remembered stood by the lake shore, and was sitting there with her eyes narrowed against the water's sunny glint, waiting for the scrambling clutch of emotions she was suffering to calm down so that she could try to think.

About what? she asked herself tartly. About why you are here? About what you want to do next? You keep refusing to examine why you are here, and you don't have a clue what you want to do next.

A maid appeared beside the bench, arriving panting, as if she'd come down here at a run. 'Signor Francesco ask me to bring you this, *signora*,' she explained breathlessly, and handed Lexi her mobile phone.

It rang the instant the maid had turned and disappeared back up the path towards the house.

'You sent someone to my room to rummage through my bag for my phone,' she fired at him before he had a chance to speak.

'I went and got it for myself,' Franco informed her. 'And *don't*,' he warned, 'start lecturing me on whether striding around the house in my present condition is good for my health, because I know that it isn't. What the hell has got into you, Lexi? Why the sudden icy exit?'

Lexi wanted to tell him. In fact she wondered why she had never told him before—three and a half years ago, when it would perhaps have meant something—but she'd run away from facing him with his unfaithfulness that time too.

'The past is catching up with me,' she mumbled, and wished she had not heard the thickness of tears threatening her voice. 'And you won't let me talk about it.'

'Don't start crying, *cara*,' he warned huskily. 'I will be

forced to come down there to you if you do. I know we have to talk about the past.'

Rolling her lips together to try and stop them from trembling, she asked, 'Can I talk about Marco too?'

'No,' he rasped.

'Your relationship with Claudia, then?'

'Claudia and I do not have a relationship,' he denied impatiently. 'Not the kind you are implying anyway.'

Lexi watched the pair of resident white swans move across the glass smooth surface of the lake, leaving triangular ripples in their wake. Swans mated with the same partner for life, she recalled, for some reason only the convoluted inner workings of her own mind could follow. It took a lot of care and trust to be so steadfast and loyal to one person.

Something that she and Franco had never had.

'I hate you,' she whispered, which seemed to tie in somehow with the thoughts preceding it.

'No, you don't. You hate yourself for still caring about me when you don't want to care. Come back up here to me and we will talk about that if you want,' he encouraged.

Lexi gave a slow mute shake of her head.

'I saw that,' he sighed.

'From where?' Jumping to her feet, Lexi spun round, expecting to find him walking down the path towards her, but she saw nothing but garden and leafy tree branches.

'From my bedroom window.'

Looking up, Lexi tracked her eyes along the upper terrace until she found his window. Her breathing pulled to a stop. She could just make out his tall figure against the long pane of glass.

'You should be lying down or something.'

'Then have some pity on me,' he said wearily. 'I ache all over, and I can do without the dramatic trip down memory lane right now, where you storm out and I have to work out what the hell I have done to cause it this time.'

But Lexi gave another shake of her head. 'You're bad for me, Franco,' she told him sadly. 'I know I shouldn't even be here with you, and…and I don't want to become attached to you again.'

*'Madre de Dio,'* he growled, then added a torrent of angry Italian that he did not know if she could follow. Switching to English, he said fiercely, 'I want you to become attached to me again! Why do you think I asked you to come back to me in the first place?'

'I don't know…'

'But you came anyway.'

Yes, she'd come anyway. 'Did you crash your boat because I'd sent you those divorce papers?'

Another set of angry curses was followed by an explosive, *'No.'*

'Then how did it happen?'

A band of pain across Franco's chest tightened, catching at his breath. He didn't want to think about that yet—not now. Perhaps later, when— 'Come back up here or I will come down there to you,' he warned again. 'In fact I am already walking towards the door—'

Watching him disappear from the window, Lexi cut the connection and started running—fast. She knew she'd been bluffed the moment she arrived in his room, to find him sprawled in the chair by the window, looking pathetically weak and endearingly bad-tempered as he waged an uneven battle with the cufflinks still anchoring his shirt cuffs to his wrists.

'Help me with these,' he ground out in frustration, cutting short whatever she'd been about to say to him as he slumped back in the chair and closed his eyes as if the small task had exhausted him.

Crossing the room to his side, she squatted down. 'Is your vision still bad?' she queried, taking hold of his wrist so she could work the first gold link free.

'No,' he grunted, annoyed that she could be so damn perceptive. 'What made you just walk out?'

'I don't like the rules you've set up around here.' Having freed that cufflink, she made him wince when she reached across him to lift up his other wrist—the one on his injured side. 'If you can allow a visit from Claudia then I don't see why you can't let in the rest of your friends and family as well.'

'Claudia is a special case—*ouch*,' he complained.

'Sorry,' Lexi said. 'I accept that she has to be a special case, but...' Her hair was getting in her way as she bent over the task in hand, and she paused to loop the long tresses back behind her ear, meeting Franco's fingers as they arrived to do the same thing. Like an idiot, she glanced up and caught the full power of his glowing dark gaze as the back of his fingers stroked against her warm cheek. Sensation erupted with a swirling coil of sensual heat low down in her belly.

'But what?' he prompted distractedly.

Lexi struggled to remember what she had been going to say. In fact she was struggling to think of anything other than that look in his eyes that she knew so well. 'Your rules are irrationally selective,' she managed to finish. 'Or is it just me you don't want to discuss the accident and Marco with?'

'I need a shower. Care to join me?' he invited softly, gently stroking her hair back behind her ear so that she quivered.

More blocking tactics, she thought, and decided to ignore him for a change. Frowning, she dragged her attention back to releasing the second cufflink, then she sighed, sitting back on her heels and thereby removing herself from his easy reach.

In a way it was a mistake: it gave him leave to run his eyes over the green print summer dress she had changed into, its short swirly skirt leaving a lot of naked leg on show.

That coil of heat tightened its grip on her. 'Stop looking at me like that.' Getting up, she turned away from him.

'Like what?'

'Like you have the strength to do what you're thinking.'

'You believe I'm too feeble to at least try?'

Walking across the room to lay the cufflinks down on top of a glossy wooden chest of drawers, Lexi turned and leant back against it, folding her arms. 'Tell me why you brought me to Italy,' she demanded up front.

At first she thought he was not going to answer. His silence stretched along with the steady way he was looking at her. Then he eased out a controlled sigh and heaved himself to his feet so he could slip off the shirt. The moment he did so Lexi began to feel vulnerable, as if she was suddenly being placed under threat. Yet what could he do to her? He might like to believe he was physically able to take on the seduction of a protesting woman, but she could see he was already swaying on his feet.

He was like a man of two halves, she found herself thinking. One half darkly, painfully battered and bruised; the other half pure, golden male, glowing with robust health. Even the dark bruising did not detract from what she could see was all attractively smooth and tight. He'd bulked out in the years since she'd last seen him like this, she observed, running her gaze over his wide shoulders, then his bulging pectoral muscles and the beautifully ridged stomach, unaware that her breathing had shortened or that her fingers were clenching and unclenching where she held them tucked away beneath her arms.

'I had an epiphany.'

Blinking rapidly in an attempt to clear her head, Lexi dragged her eyes back up to his face, saw he'd been watching her look at him, and felt guilty heat pour into her face.

'Excuse me?' she murmured.

His dark eyes narrowed, glinting knowingly, 'An epiphany,' he repeated. 'About my life and what I wanted to do with it.'

An epiphany… Rolling the tip of her tongue over her lips,

Lexi straightened up and dropped her arms to her sides—though she wasn't sure why she needed to do it. 'And this epiphany told you what?'

'That it was time to win my wife back,' he enlightened her. 'Time to put aside the bad stuff and get our marriage back on track.'

'It was never on track—'

'To place our marriage on a good solid track, then.' The flick of a hand tossed semantics to one side.

'Stay where you are,' Lexi told him jerkily when he started crossing the space separating them. 'When—when did you have this epiphany?'

'Does it matter?' He didn't stop walking.

'Yes.' Lexi knew why she'd straightened up now. Even battered and bruised Franco could be incredibly intimidating—if only because her senses liked it when he came over all domineering and broodingly macho.

'When I finally accepted how miserable I was without you.'

'Y-you were even more miserable with me,' she reminded him, feeling one of the rounded brass knobs on the chest of drawers dig into her back as she backed off more the closer he came.

'I know. That is why I called it an epiphany.' He came to a stop six inches away. 'Like a sudden leap of intuitive understanding that told me I was miserable with you but more miserable without you.' He added a small descriptive shrug. 'It is as simple and as crazy as that.'

'You said it.' Wishing she could stop looking at his half bruised, hair roughened torso, she asked tartly, 'Were you suffering from another epiphany when you had Claudia clasped to your wounded chest?'

'That was sympathy.'

'Show *me* some, then, and take a long step back.'

'So you can escape?'

'Yes,' Lexi nodded. 'You know I won't physically make you do it when you're all bruised like that.'

'Ah—you are attempting to appeal to my sense of fair play?'

Lexi pressed her lips together and nodded her head again. If there was one thing she knew for absolute certain about Franco it was his sporting sense of fair play.

'Look at me, then—up here where my eyes are.' He indicated with the movement of one of his hands. 'Just one brief eye to eye contact, *cara*, and I promise I will step back.'

Thinking it was a bit like asking her to strip naked—because making eye contact with Franco had much the same effect on her already edgy senses—Lexi pushed out a short sigh then lifted up her chin.

He dared to smile, with his lips and his eyes—a tender kind of gentle humour that struck like a flaming arrow directly at her heart. 'I wish you weren't so handsome,' she told him wistfully. 'Why couldn't you have a bigger nose, or something? Or a fat, ugly mouth?'

'You know...' Reaching out to run his hands around her slender waist, he carefully drew her closer. 'Your open honesty will shame the devil one day.'

'Are you the devil in question?' She didn't even try to stop her progress towards him.

Franco grimaced. 'Probably... I suppose—yes...' he admitted. 'Because I am about to break my promise to you, and...' He did not bother to finish the sentence; he just closed the gap between their mouths.

It was like taking flight without wings to help her control her take-off, and the worst thing was she didn't even try to put up a fight. She was just a pathetic pushover, she told herself, moving closer until she felt the tips of her breasts catch hold of the heat emanating from his chest, parting her lips and sighing a helpless little sigh he caught with the sensual dip of his tongue. He kissed her until she melted against him, until she was mimicking his tongue with her own and feeling the rise of desire, tasting it like some rare, delicious fruit you could only obtain from this one source. As she let her hands drift upwards to stroke the firm muscles and smooth skin covering his arms she felt a fine tremor run through him.

Dangerous, she tried to tell herself. This—him—us.

And then she tasted the lipstick. Claudia's lipstick. It had to be Claudia's because she wasn't wearing any. And that, she thought as she pulled her head back, was the reason why being anywhere near Franco was dangerous. He could warm her right through and contrarily chill her to her bone at the same time.

His eyes narrowed at her sudden withdrawal. Lexi feathered down her own eyelashes so he could not pierce into her thoughts.

'May I go now?' she requested coolly.

Tension was suddenly flashing between them, like microwaves probing deep into her flesh, and she almost wilted with relief when he recovered his sense of fair play, dropping his arms from her and taking the promised step back.

Mouth dry, heart just an aching squeeze in her chest, without saying another word Lexi stepped around him and walked out of the room.

Watching her depart, Franco was still puzzling over what had turned her off like that when he raised a set of fingers to his kiss warmed mouth. Something made him glance down. He saw the red lipstick he'd forgotten to wipe away after Claudia's kisses—and let loose a string of soft curses aimed exclusively at himself for being such a thoughtless, insensitive swine.

For the next twenty-four hours Lexi avoided him. She didn't even go to his room to protest that he'd had her moved to the suite next door to his. Zeta took him meals to tempt his appetite, only to bring them back again barely touched, and she

informed Lexi she was worried because he was too exhausted
to eat. The housekeeper complained that he was working up
there on his laptop and refusing to lie down to rest on his bed.
She conveyed her displeasure to Lexi, who spent the evening
curled up on a sofa watching television and didn't seem to
care what he was doing.

Lexi was training herself not to care.

When it was time for bed she went to her new room without bothering to go in and check how he was. She just pulled
on one of her new silk nighties and slipped between the cool
linen sheets, switched off the lights and willed herself to
sleep. The next morning she walked several circuits of the
lake after breakfast, stopping to coax the resident swans with
some bread she'd stolen from the breakfast table. She knew
that Franco was standing on the upper terrace watching her;
though she didn't once glimpse his tall figure standing there
the couple of times she allowed herself to glance up.

She had her mobile phone tucked into one of the pockets
of the flowery dress she'd put on with its fashionably fitted
bodice and full skirt.

But he didn't call her.

It was like a war of attrition. The problem was that Lexi
knew she was waging this particular war all by herself. She
wanted to avoid him but she wanted him to call her. Where
was the sense in that?

She thought he might come down for lunch, but he didn't.
She hoped he would arrive when Zeta served her afternoon
tea on the lower terrace overlooking the lake, but was informed by the satisfied housekeeper that at last he was sleeping on his bed and the laptop was shut.

By dinner time Lexi was losing the battle—the part that
was supposed to be training her to stop caring about him,
anyway—and she knew, just *knew*, she was about to give in.
It came over her like one of those uncontrollable rushes of
weakness that made you do nonsensical things. She'd gone

up to her room to wash and change before dinner, but found herself hovering outside his door instead.

Zeta had told her he was still sleeping. Taking a quick peek at him while he slept wasn't the same as going in there cold, so to speak, having to face him with her own weakness, she convinced herself.

But it was just the same, and Lexi knew it even as she twisted the handle and pushed open the door. She knew it as she stepped inside and closed the door behind her, leaning against it and breathing fast, as if she was a naughty child up to mischief. Dusk had fallen and the twin lamps beside the bed cast gentle light across the room. The long windows stood open to the soft evening breeze coming in from the garden, and as she breathed in she caught the clean scent of his soap in her nostrils before she allowed herself to look towards the bed.

He wasn't there. Her heart started to pump that bit faster. His bathroom door stood open, so she could see that he wasn't in there. Aware that her limbs had acquired a spongy sensation, making her feel nervously strung out, she pushed away from the door and walked across the room to the only other place she could think he might be.

Stepping outside onto the terrace, she found him sitting on one of the chairs out there with his long legs stretched out in front of him, his feet resting on another chair. He was dressed in pale chinos and a soft pale blue cambric shirt. No socks inside the casual slip-ons he wore on his golden brown feet. On the table beside him stood an uncorked bottle of red wine and two long-stemmed glasses. As he heard her step and turned his dark head to look at her Lexi knew by his steady regard that it was game over.

He knew that she knew she was giving up the fight—with herself.

# CHAPTER SEVEN

HE RAISED his hand and held it out to her. That was all it took to draw her to him. Lexi walked the few metres and placed her hand in his. His fingers closed around her fingers, warm, slightly callused, strong.

'Glass of wine?' he asked her.

'Please,' she said, but it was barely a whisper that scraped over her dry throat.

Dropping his feet to the floor he stood up. She noticed straight away that his movements were smooth and lithe— pain free. As if he'd planned everything down to the smallest detail he drew her closer to his side, slid her captured hand around his waist then let go of it so he could pour out the wine without them losing physical contact.

He handed her a glass, which she took with her other hand. 'To us,' he said, and chinked their glasses together, then waited like some powerful dark force for her to raise her glass to her lips.

'To us—or now.' Lexi found she had just enough fight left in her to extend the toast before she raised the glass and sipped from it.

It took him a moment or two to accept what she'd said before he lifted his own glass and drank.

In some dark place inside her Lexi knew she wanted to weep. Maybe he could sense it. Maybe he was aware that no matter how much she wanted him she did not want *this*. Because he released a small sigh, placed his glass back on the table and took her glass to do the same thing with it, then turned to take her fully into his arms.

'One small step at a time, hmm?' he murmured, alongside the kiss he pressed to the top of her silky head.

Lexi lifted her face to look at him, the swirling blue-green in her eyes mocking him for saying such a thing when they both knew that what was going to happen next was not going to be anything like a small step. And, anyway, she had already taken a huge step just by coming here to him, so thinking small did not come close to where she wanted to go with this.

'Of course if small is all you can manage right now...' she posed, in an attempt to make light of things.

Franco laughed—not a throw-back-his-head kind of laugh, but a low down, deep-into-his-chest kind of sexy, dark and very masculine laugh. 'I don't know what I'm up for,' he confessed with rueful honesty, 'though we could make it interesting finding out...'

Lexi turned to release a small, slightly shaky laugh. Franco felt some of the tension ease out of her slender frame. He felt the same easing out of himself. He'd achieved something here he hadn't dared expect to achieve. He'd brought down her defences without needing to touch on all the ugly stuff still waiting in the background for its moment to shatter them both.

Whether that was being fair to her or not he did not want to consider right now. She was here. She was acknowledging that she wanted—no, *needed* to be here with him. He turned with her still pressed against him and walked them both inside.

In the soft light of the room he drew her round in front of him and, as if it was the most natural thing for them to do, their lips came together to embrace. She stepped in that bit closer, lifted her slender arms and slid them around his neck. As he buried his fingers in the loose silken flow of her hair he caught her soft whisper just before she took the initiative and deepened the kiss to an open-mouthed probe of hungry passion that unfurled her longing for him like an exquisite flowering that made her ache.

Her cheeks were flushed when eventually he eased back from her; a terrible shyness Lexi had not experienced even the first time she'd been with him kept her eyes fixed on the open collar of his shirt, and the feelings dancing around inside her made her feel quivery and weak. 'I suppose we should go down and eat dinner f-first,' she heard herself mumble.

'Bailing out on me already?' he quizzed.

Not so you would notice, Lexi thought as he trailed his fingers down the length of her back. It was enough to make her body arch into closer contact with him.

'Zeta will come looking for me if I don't go down.'

His answer to that problem was to step back from her and stride across the room to pick up the house phone. The husky lowness of his voice as he spoke to the housekeeper fired up the heat in Lexi's face.

'Now she knows what we're doing,' she protested as he walked back to her.

'We are man and wife. Holding back dinner while we make love is not a hanging offence.'

'Yes, but—'

He stopped walking. 'You want to eat first?'

Oh, for goodness' sake, Lexi thought hectically. She didn't know what she wanted! 'I want to be with you but I don't want to be with you!' The confession arrived as a cry from the heart.

'I know that,' he answered gently.

'I w-want to go home to London and forget all about you but I can't make myself do it!'

'I know that too.'

'And—and asking me if I want to eat first like we're making a date for sex isn't helping me here!'

'Then I will rephrase the question. Do you want to eat, make love or fight?'

None of them—all of them! Throwing up her hands in an agitated gesture of confused defeat, she let her blue-green eyes flicker over him. He stood about three feet away, exuding the grave patience of a saint. Her man. Her lover. Her only lover! Married to him. His ring circled her finger. His name had become her name almost four years ago; yet she couldn't recall a single time that she'd used it outside Italy.

'We were so young,' she breathed, for some reason she couldn't follow right now. 'Nineteen and twenty-four when we met, Franco. It should have been the great holiday romance of a lifetime and ended at that.'

'But it didn't.'

'No.' Folding her arms, Lexi hugged herself tightly. 'We got pregnant.'

A pained look passed across his face and he lifted up that hand again. 'Lexi—'

'We are still young,' she whispered with a shake of her head. 'I should be out clubbing every night and—and trying out different men for the hell of it. And you should be out there sowing wild oats all over the place and—and crashing your super-macho boats.'

That made him laugh. Lexi didn't blame him, she almost laughed herself, but... 'This—epiphany you had about us,' she posed unsteadily. 'It could collapse into rubble once you've got over the accident and sorted out your emotions about Marco.'

'What was your epiphany?'

Lexi blinked at him. 'I didn't have one. You did.'

'Then why are you here with me right now, *cara*. What drove you back here into my life?'

Hearing just one tiny four-letter word whisper its powerful song in her head sent the tip of her tongue in an anxious flurry across her trembling upper lip. 'You were hurt—'

'I am healing. You are still here.' Heaving out a sigh, he started moving again, closing the gap between them so he could take hold of her defensively folded arms and prise them apart. 'I have made a decision. We go downstairs and eat dinner like a respectable old married couple without an ounce of gloriously impulsive passion left.'

'You're angry with me?'

'No,' he denied, trailing her out onto the landing. 'I am trying my best to give you what you feel you need right now.'

'Aggro and frustration?'

'If the label fits, Lexi.'

Lexi tried to tug to a standstill outside her bedroom door. 'I need to change and...'

'You look amazing as you are,' Franco informed her. 'All sun-kissed and healthy after the amount of exercise you have been expending beside the lake, trying to stop yourself from coming to me.'

'So you *were* watching me.' She sighed as he drew her with him down the stairs.

'Each wistful sigh, each stubborn shake of your beautiful head, each furtive glance to check if I was standing there.'

'I didn't see you.'

'I hid like a spy on secret surveillance.'

They entered the small dining room to be greeted by the flickering light from candles and the sight of the table already set for two.

Lexi pulled to a stop. 'You were coming down for dinner?'

'Mmm,' he murmured, 'but you came to visit me and spoiled my surprise.'

She'd given in too soon. That was what he was saying. If

she'd hung out just a little bit longer she could have saved herself a soul crunching loss of pride.

Zeta arrived then, coming to a halt in surprise when she saw the two of them. 'I thought you said—'

'We changed our minds,' Franco cut in ruefully. 'Apparently, at the age of twenty-eight, I am too old for impulsive bursts of lusty passion.'

Lexi flushed up to the roots of her shining hair and sent him a glowering glance. He just laughed huskily as he politely held out one of the chairs for her, then brushed a kiss across her hot cheek before he took the other chair.

Watching the way he moved, Lexi was becoming more aware of the difference a short twenty-four hours had made in him. His colour was good—fabulous, actually, she amended, watching the candlelight catch the lean golden contours of his face.

They ate their food and indulged in minor light dinner table talk, which was fine so long as she kept her vision slightly out of focus when she looked at him. However, there was nothing light about what was prowling around them, like a hungry tiger waiting for its moment to pounce on them both.

'Tell me about these dozens of men you've been testing out while clubbing,' he invited suddenly.

Now, there was an exaggeration if ever there was one, Lexi mused grimacingly, 'It's bad taste to kiss and tell,' she deflected smoothly.

'Dayton must disapprove.'

Lexi watched the candlelight flicker across the long stemmed, crystal glass she was fingering and felt a twinge of guilt over Bruce. 'Bruce has just gone on the banned list,' she stated flatly.

'But he is such a major part of your life—'

'Are you ready to talk about Marco?' She shot the challenge from the hip and watched his expression shut down like a door slamming shut across his face.

'No.'

'Why not?'

'Tell me about your childhood.'

Lexi pulled a face as that imaginary door slammed a second time. 'Not much to tell.' Reaching out, she spooned up a portion of Zeta's homemade crème caramel and placed it in a dish. 'I lived the first ten years of my life with my grandmother—'

'Where was your mother?' Franco frowned.

'Working,' Lexi said. 'It's the nature of the acting beast. She was in touring rep a lot then, and living out of a suitcase, so my grandmother brought me up. When she died, Grace had to take over caring for me, which basically meant leaving me in the care of a succession of friends in different cities while she had to work.'

'That sounds much like the succession of nannies who had the pleasure of bringing me up after my mother died,' Franco murmured.

'Oh, poor little rich boy,' Lexi teased him. 'Your father thinks the absolute world of you and you know it.'

'He was busy. He adored me when he had the time. If I wasn't rattling around this huge place on my own, I was living in at a boarding school for rich kids.'

'Is that where you met Marco?' Lexi dared.

It didn't gain her anything but the sight of his lips snapping together, before he parted them again and said, 'We were talking about *your* childhood.'

'Well, I didn't make many friends.' She grimaced. 'It's kind of difficult to form lasting friendships when you're forever on the move like a travelling circus. Here—try some of this…' Spooning up a portion of the dessert, she placed the dish in front of him. 'It's the most delicious thing I've tasted in years.'

'So which did you prefer? The travelling circus or living with your grandmother?' he probed, lifting up his spoon.

'Oh, my grandmother,' Lexi responded instantly. 'She was a bit strict—scared, I think, that I might turn out to be what she called "frivolous" like Grace, but overall we got on well together.'

'And your father? Did he have no part to play in your life back then?'

A part to play? She would have had to know who he was for him to have done that. 'Why are you asking me all these questions about my past?' she asked him, frowning as she sat back in her chair. 'You were never interested about where I came from before.'

'That is why I am asking now.'

'Well, don't.' Sitting forward again, she spooned up some of the crème caramel but couldn't quite make herself lift it to her mouth. So she laid it back in the dish, glanced up, saw the way he was studying her. The shimmering glint going on between those sooty eyelashes made her feel more prickly the longer his scrutiny went on.

'What?' she snapped when she could stand it no longer, defiant and defensive at the same time.

'I think I have inadvertently hit a tender nerve,' he drawled slowly.

'No. I just don't understand your sudden interest.'

'You are my wife—'

'Estranged wife.' Why did that sound so wrong right now? Reaching out to pick up her wine glass, Lexi sat glaring into its contents. So they were sitting here, eating a meal together like husband and wife. So they were intending to go from here to the same bed and—well—do what married couples usually did and sleep together—in every sense. Half an hour ago they'd almost missed dinner and headed straight for the bed. But none of the above made them a married couple, and definitely did not make him a husband and her a wife.

It never had the last time she'd lived here as his wife. She'd been plonked in a suite two wings away from him like some bad germ it was best to keep as far away from him as possible. And he hadn't complained. He hadn't kicked up a fuss or had her moved to the suite next door to him like he'd done this time. He'd visited her like a reluctant but rigidly polite host, with polite knocks on her door and polite enquiries as to her health, every single morning before he'd left for work, she recalled; and she felt the same bleak emptiness fill her now that had used to fill her up back then.

He'd looked so tall and breathtakingly handsome, wearing a business suit that had made him look oddly younger—when it should have been the other way round. Because the guy who'd lived in shorts and a T-shirt all through the summer should have looked the younger one.

'Lexi...' he prompted softly.

'I don't have a father,' she announced.

'Everyone has a father, *cara*,' he drawled.

'Well, I don't. Now, change the subject.'

He was lounging back in his chair now, which placed his face out of the flickering light from the candles so she couldn't read his expression. But she could feel the cogs in his brain turning over, feel him pondering whether to push her a bit more into opening up for him.

Then he took in a short breath. 'If it upsets you this much then I offer you my apologies,' he said smoothly. 'I agree. Let's change the subject.'

But now he was willing to do that Lexi found herself changing her mind too. 'No. Let's finish what you've already started and get it over with. So what do you want to know. My full family tree? OK.' She sat back again, tense as a skittish cat and defiant with it. She tossed her hair back from her face. 'Mother—Grace Hamilton. Actress but not famous.' She lifted her hand up to place Grace like an imaginary branch in the air in front of her, her fingers trembling as she did. 'Father—unknown. Because Grace was very vague about things she did not want to face and there was no name on my birth certificate.' She placed him in the air next to Grace. 'Oh, and I forgot to put my grandmother up there. Anyone else?' She pretended to ponder that, with her eyes flashing all kinds of aggression, while Franco just reclined back in his chair and listened with an infuriatingly impassive silence. 'A hamster called Racket,' she remembered. 'I wanted a dog, but I wasn't allowed one because we moved around too much. Then there is Bruce, of course.' As she spoke Bruce's name she dared Franco with the sparkle in her eyes to say a single thing. 'Bruce is the only person who has ever been and remained a constant part of my life...I wonder where I should place him on my tree?'

'Father figure?' Franco suggested, with a silken stealth that raised Lexi's hackles so much she thought for a second she was going to leap up and hit him.

'You need to wash your mouth out with soap.' She made do with sending him a withering glance. 'At least he's always cared what happened to me.'

'And lusted after you like a seething old lecher.'

'How dare you say that?' Lexi gasped out.

'I dare because he is twelve years older than you, yet he could never look at you without stripping your clothes off.'

Stung by that shocking observation, she hit right back. 'Well, better a sleazy old lecher than a two-timing young one.'

Franco's dark head went back. 'Are you calling me a lecher?'

'What do you call a guy who pursues a stupid, innocent girl with the sole intention of bedding her for a bet?'

'The bet was—unfortunate,' he growled, with an impatient movement of his hand that Lexi read as downright haunted guilt. 'It had nothing to do with what you and I were really about.'

'Tell that to your golden friends.' Lexi laughed, and it

wasn't a nice laugh. 'And let us not gloss over the fact that you collected your winnings,' she added for good measure.

'There was a reason why I did that,' he said tightly.

'I'm all ears,' encouraged Lexi.

'We were discussing Bruce Dayton's unhealthy obsession with you,' he muttered, losing all that super cool sophistication he'd brought to the dinner table.

'Bruce has been good to me.'

'The perfect father figure.'

'Stop calling him that. He's not old enough to be my father!'

'Uncle then,' Franco amended. 'Whatever—it was sick.'

Her cheeks gone pale now, Lexi thrust her chin up. 'The way *you* treated me was sick, Franco.'

He surprised her by backing right off from that accusation. Getting up from the table, he strode across the room towards the drinks cabinet, and Lexi could feel him inwardly cursing the fact that he was limping again. 'If I tell you I am deeply ashamed that I allowed that bet to stand, will you just let it go now?'

Well, *could* she let it go?

He'd turned around and was watching her with the intent expression of a man who genuinely meant what he'd just said. It some ways Lexi knew that this was a big moment in the strange up-and-down relationship they'd been having since she'd come back into his life—though it wasn't the biggest, most crucial moment.

'Seeing you accept that bet broke my heart,' she told him bleakly.

'I'm sorry,' he said heavily, then sighed because he knew that sounded inadequate after what she'd just confessed. 'Claudia was a jealous cat, and she aimed to hurt you deeply when she sent that video clip to your phone.'

She'd known that. Even back then she'd understood

Claudia's motives, though understanding them had not soft-ened the pain she'd suffered.

'She too was deeply ashamed of the part she'd played in hurting you,' Franco went on soberly. 'Especially so when you lost your mother not long afterwards and—'

'The rest of my world came tumbling down,' Lexi completed for him. Then she heaved in a breath, let it out again, and stood up. 'I forgive you both for the bet, OK?' she announced stiffly. 'I will even forgive you for turning so cold on me the week before the bet came to light, and for hating being married to me. After all—' she released a jerky laugh '—I hated you just as much by then. But what I refuse to forgive,' she added, a flush of anger rising to her cheeks, 'is you enjoying yourself with Claudia in our bed in our apartment while I was in hospital miscarrying our baby. And now I think I will go alone to bed.'

'Just hold on a minute.' As if she'd just shot a stray bullet at him, Franco tensed. 'That last part did not happen!'

'Telephones with cameras are the bastards of intrusion,' Lexi mocked as she crossed the room at speed to the door. 'And trust me, Franco,' she couldn't resist launching at him once she'd got there, 'whatever people like to say to the contrary, cameras don't tell lies!'

'Lexi—come back here!' he raked out as she flung herself out of the room at full pelt, because she'd caught the warning spark of blistering fury lighting up the gold in his eyes.

She was halfway up the stairs when she heard the crash, then a string of angry curses. 'I hope that was you falling on your lying face!' she stopped to yell down at him. 'And so much for getting to know each other, Francesco! Great trip down memory lane—thanks!'

She didn't even see Zeta standing in the hall, staring after her in appalled dismay as she raced up the rest of the stairs. Franco saw the housekeeper, though, when she appeared in the open doorway to a string of vicious curses as he got up from the floor, rubbing his thigh. One of the dining chairs lay on its side because he'd tripped over it, and the bottle of wine he'd been holding in his hand was lying next to it, dripping its red contents onto the polished oak floor.

'Don't say a damn word,' he growled at the housekeeper when she opened her mouth to speak.

'But—did she do this to you?'

'My wife can do anything she wants to me,' he responded harshly, gripping his shoulder because he'd wrenched it trying to break his fall. 'She can put a loaded gun to my head and pull the trigger if she feels like it. It is her right, her prerogative…damn!' he cursed when he tried to put his weight on his injured leg and almost collapsed again.

Zeta came hurrying forward, but he waved her back. 'I'm OK,' he muttered less forcefully. 'Just get out of here, Zeta. This is private between me and Lexi, and we don't need witnesses while we make fools of ourselves.'

Lexi didn't feel foolish; she felt like a bubbling mass of boiling fury.

What was she doing here?'

It was all out now. The door in her head was standing wide open and everything was spilling out right in front of her: the hurt, the betrayal, all as fresh and raw as if it was only just happening. She wanted to curl up in a corner and cry her eyes out, but she also wanted to run back down there and spit out some more accusations at the man she hated so much right now it physically hurt!

Wife…what a miserable joke, she thought painfully, looking around the suite that was so similar to the suite she'd used to have—if she didn't count the several corridors in between. Different colour coordination, different view from the window, but right now it felt just like the same luxury prison cell that had doubled as her only place of sanctuary from the cold comfort offered to her!

Grimly she stripped her clothes off, dragged her nightie

on over her head, crawled beneath the cool linen sheets and then curled up in a tight ball. She was trembling—all over. Shivering and shaking with a huge lump of tears growing in her throat like an inflating balloon. To think she'd almost gone to bed with him. To think she'd convinced herself she was ready to let the past go.

Her bedroom door flew open. She knew it was Franco. 'If you've come to ask politely after my health, then don't bother!' she launched at him from the depths of the sheet she'd pulled over her head.

His disconcerted stillness sizzled across the darkened room.

'And you forgot to knock!'

'What the hell are you talking about now?' he fired back.

'Tell me…' Fighting with the sheet so she could sit up, Lexi yanked her hair back from where it had tumbled across her hot face. He was standing there, lit by the light on the landing, a huge great dark silhouette that still managed to look disgustingly gorgeous. 'Were you sent by your father to check on me each morning?'

'Sent to check on you?' Naturally he didn't know what she was talking about, since he had not been privy to her thoughts.

'The last time I lived here,' she enlightened him. 'I had this—' she gave a flick with her hand '—this image of your father, ordering you upstairs to my room to check on my health every morning before you both left for Livorno. You used to knock so politely, then stand there in the doorway—just like you're doing now—and look at me like you wished I wasn't there…'

Franco stiffened as if she'd leapt up and slapped his face. 'I was not ordered upstairs and I never wished you were not here!' he denied harshly.

'Man and wife with bedrooms five miles apart?' Lexi muttered in a thick voice that shook. 'You didn't bother to have me moved then, did you? You liked having three quarters of this stupid house between us.'

She heard his sigh as he walked towards the bed, and knew he'd caught the tremor of hurt in her voice.

'I was out of my comfort zone,' he confessed heavily. 'You did not say anything about where you were sleeping, and I didn't know how to broach the subject without sounding like an oversexed monster eager to have you close enough to jump on when I felt like it, so I left it alone.'

'You didn't want to jump on me.'

He said nothing.

'And I would have needed nerves of steel to complain about my accommodation when I knew how much you hated me.'

'You hated me too, Lexi…'

She sighed at that comeback, because it was only the truth, and he sighed too, then lowered himself down to sit on the edge of her bed. Lexi saw him wince, saw him lay a hand on his injured thigh, wished she didn't love and hate him at the same time. Then she almost choked on the sob she had to fight back when it hit her that she did—still love him. Oh, what a pig!

'What do you want me to say? That I made a mess of the whole thing? OK, I made a mess of the whole thing,' he admitted. 'I believed…' He stopped, causing a sting of a rift to open up while Lexi sat waiting for him to finish. When he did continue she got the feeling he'd carefully rethought what he wanted to say. 'I let…other people dictate to me how I should be thinking and feeling about you. But I never wished you gone—ever.'

The tagged on *ever* rang like a low-sounding bass bell, striking out dark, intense sincerity.

'I used to cry into my pillow each morning after you'd left.' She wasn't looking at him now, but down at her fingers where they crushed the sheet. 'I wanted so badly for my mother to walk into that bedroom and sweep me up in her arms and carry me away from here.'

'Lexi…' he growled unsteadily.

But Lexi just shook her head against whatever that unsteady 'Lexi' was meant to relay. 'You'd turned cold on me before we married. Before Grace died, before I learnt about that stupid bet. Knowing that, I should not have married you.'

Grinding out a soft curse, he reached to grasp her twisting fingers. 'Look, I'm really sorry about the bet. I mean it. I'm sorry. I was an arrogant fool. I believed something someone told me about you and I—I wanted to hit back at you, so I… collected my—my winnings, knowing that Claudia was recording the moment and that she was likely to send it to you.'

'You believed something someone told you about me?' Lifting up her head Lexi looked at him. 'What something?'

But he just frowned and shook his head, 'Let's talk about convenient cameras and sex romps that did not happen.'

Being reminded of that, Lexi tugged her fingers free and threw herself back down on the pillows. 'No. Go away,' she muttered, and pulled the sheet over her head.

Without any warning whatsoever that it was going to happen, Franco lost his temper. The next thing she knew she lying pinned beneath his weight, because he'd stretched out on top of her like a wrestler, pinning her to the bed.

'Talk,' he rasped, tugging the sheet down so he could glower at her. 'Because I did not sleep with Claudia. I have never slept with Claudia! I want to know why you ever believed that I did!'

If she hadn't seen the proof for herself Lexi would have started to believe him. He looked so offended. Bright golden flames of denial were leaping in his eyes.

'Where were you the night they took me to hospital?' she challenged icily.

'Blind drunk in a bar in town somewhere,' he answered

instantly. 'Too sloshed to know what I was doing and too miserable about us to care.'

'I called you—four times!' Accusing sparks flew from her eyes now. 'You didn't even bother to answer me—not once!'

Franco tried to recall what else he'd been doing while he'd drunk himself into a forgetful stupor that night. 'Marco found me and took me home,' he recounted. 'I could barely walk in a straight line. He put me to bed. I don't remember any phone calls. I don't remember anything much about that night.'

'So Claudia hid in a cupboard, waiting to jump out once you were naked and comatose on the bed, then jumped on you?'

He looked stunned. 'You saw that?'

'Of course I saw that!' Lexi tried to wriggle out from beneath him.

'Stay still,' he muttered. 'I'm hurting all over as it is.'

To her annoyance, she went perfectly still beneath him. 'Do you think I enjoy making up fantasies where my so-called husband gets passionate with another woman in our bed while I'm—?'

'Whose phone?' he cut in, and she could feel all the muscles in him tensing.

'Claudia's phone. Though how she managed to take pictures of what you were both up to while—what?' Lexi said as his face drained of colour, his eyes turning that horrible black onyx.

He didn't answer. Something about the way he suddenly rolled away from her to land on his feet by the bed and then just stood there stone still, staring at nothing, made Lexi sit up again, with a funny feeling of alarm crawling around in her chest.

'Franco?' she prompted uncertainly.

Franco didn't even hear her. A red mist had risen across his eyes, in the centre of which was an image Marco had planted there of him twined in the throes of passion with Lexi. But the twined couple he was seeing right now was himself with Claudia, as described by Lexi, who had been sent that image by—

As if he was drunk out of his head for the first time since the night Lexi had lost their baby Franco moved across the room and out of it without saying another single word.

# CHAPTER EIGHT

LEXI sat hugging her knees and stared after him, aware that something terribly dramatic had happened here—only she just didn't know what it was.

He'd looked—shattered.

Was that her fault? A guilty squirm struck down the curve of her backbone. She was supposed to be here to take care of him, not to get into fights with him every five minutes. She was supposed to be sensitive to his fragile mental state.

Marco... He'd actually talked about Marco just before he—

Scrambling out of the bed, she ran after him. The guilty feeling worsened when she found him sitting on the edge of his own bed with his face buried in his hands.

'Franco?' She went to drop down in front of him. 'Are you all right?'

For a few seconds he didn't move or say anything. Feeling that clutch of concern growing inside her, Lexi reached up and gently threaded her fingers between the spread of his own fingers, then tugged them away from his face.

'I'm OK,' he husked.

Well, he didn't look OK. The grey cast was back, strain carving out each feature, as if he was labouring under some terrible shock. And the most disturbing thing of all was that she thought she could see the burn of tears lurking behind the awful haunted look in his eyes. As if he knew what she was seeing, he lowered his heavy black lustrous eyelashes and swallowed, following it up by clearing his throat. She still held his hands, so she could feel a slight tremor running through them.

Was he finally giving in to his grief for Marco?

'I'm sorry if I went too far fighting with you,' she whispered contritely. 'I keep forgetting you're—'

'Off my head?' he offered, when she hesitated over saying something similar.

'Unwell,' Lexi substituted, making a half smile tilt the corners of his tensely held mouth.

'Sick, crazy, stupid, blind…' he offered as other alternatives.

'Is your eyesight still not good?' she asked sharply. 'Is that why you had a fight with the furniture downstairs?'

It seemed to Franco to be as good an excuse as any to leave her with. Better that than the truth anyway. 'I think I might have done some damage to the wound in my thigh,' he admitted.

She looked down at his legs, her dusky eyelashes trembling as she lifted up their clasped hands so she could scan his pale chinos for evidence of blood—but there was none. All he'd probably done was bruise it—just another one to add to the many he already had, he thought grimly.

Lexi heaved in a breath. 'Right, then, we had better take a look.' Glad to have something practical to think about other than the strange, thickly intense emotions swirling around the two of them right now, she reclaimed her hands and stood up. 'You—you'll have to take your trousers off.'

'You're intending to play nurse—dressed like that?' Franco drawled, grazing a mocking glance over her short pink nightie.

'One thing I will never be is a nurse,' Lexi returned, determined to keep this light from now on, even if it killed her, because she didn't ever want to send Franco back into that terrible dark place he'd just emerged from. 'And you've seen me wearing less, so stop complaining.'

'I was not complaining, merely making an observation.'

'Well…' The next deep breath she took felt dreadfully cluttered up. 'If you can stand up, lose the trousers, then we'll be even.'

He wasn't joking about the wound she saw once the chinos lay discarded on the bed. There was a thin trail of blood seeping through the dressing.

She chewed on her bottom lip for a second. 'So, what do we do now?'

'I remove the dressing and take a look while you fetch me a fresh one.' Sitting down again, he began to pick at the sealed edges of the white strip. 'In the bathroom, by the washbasin,' he instructed.

Lexi moved off obediently. She had a feeling he was deliberately playing things light too, because he didn't want things to kick off between them again.

How had they done that? Got so far they'd almost ended up screaming at each other?

She had screamed at him, she remembered, as she took a minute to wash her hands thoroughly before picking up the sealed sterile dressing packet and taking it back into the bedroom along with a clean towel.

'Squeamish?' he asked when she went still half a metre away.

'I don't know. I've never seen an open wound before.'

'It isn't open.'

He peeled the last of the old dressing away and she saw that he was telling the truth. A four-inch purple line was all that was left to show for the surgery, except for a tiny gape in the middle, which must be where he'd knocked it.

'That healed quickly.' Walking forward again, she sat down beside him on the bed. 'Does it hurt?'

'Not much. If you open that packet you will find a small plastic tube in there, filled with clear liquid.'

Franco took the tube from her, snapped its seal and applied the liquid to the wound. 'What does it do?' she asked curiously as she watched.

'Accelerates the healing process... You ask a lot of questions for a reluctant nurse.'

'I'm not the one doing the nursing. It's not bleeding any more...'

'There should be a clean, dry pad in the packet,' Franco prompted, and she found it and offered it to him, then watched again while he used it to soak up the excess liquid. When he was done she took it from him and silently handed him the fresh dressing strip, which he proceeded to smooth into place.

'Lexi, I'm sorry,' he murmured suddenly. 'About everything we put you through.'

The 'we' sounded odd, but she didn't pick him up on it. She was more concerned with the tension knot she could feel inside her tummy, because there was something in the way he'd made that apology that she didn't quite like.

'I was an easy target.' It was amazing, she thought, how a big row followed by a fright could bring on concessions. 'I was hateful to you most of the time.'

'With reason.'

'Yes, well...' Needing something to do, she gathered up the discarded items and stood up. 'I'll put these in the bathroom wastebin.'

'Then go back to bed.'

She stilled halfway to the bathroom, oddly wounded by the flat way he'd said that. 'Thanks for the permission,' she whispered.

'And tomorrow, if you want, you can go back to London.'

Now she knew what it felt like to be stabbed in the back. She swung round, her face paled to parchment. He was sitting there, still smoothing his long fingers over the white dressing as if he expected it to fall off if he stopped. His head was dipped. In fact she realised he hadn't looked at her properly once since she'd seen that horrible strained, haunted look when she'd pulled his hands away from his face.

'Y-you want me to leave?' Even she heard the hurt choking up her voice.

'You and I both know I'm not about to do anything stupid, Lexi,' he said grimly. 'I should not have… I used emotional blackmail to get you here, then to keep you here. Now it is time for me to start playing fair again. So I am letting you know that you can go home—no regrets.'

She hadn't expected this. After all the things they'd been throwing at each other over the last few days she just had not expected him to—to… 'S-so all that stuff about—about us trying again was what? You using me as a diversion so you didn't have to think about M-Marco?'

He rose to his feet, a frowning black scowl on his face now. 'I am just trying to play fair.'

'I don't want you to play fair!' Tears were gathering. She could feel them building in her throat. 'I want you to be honest with me and just tell me—have I been a diversion so you did not have to face your guilt and grief about Marco?'

'No!' he rasped.

'Then what?' she persisted.

Like a man driven to commit murder he strode towards her, took her by her trembling shoulders and heaved her up against his chest. 'You just don't know when it is safer to say nothing, do you?' he raked down at her angrily. 'You were like this four years ago—a yappy little temptress who never knew when to shut up!'

'Y-you said you liked me yappy back then.'

'I like you yappy now. That is the whole damn point!' He sighed when he saw her soft mouth was trembling. Her eyes looked huge and hurt and— *'Santa cielo,'* he groaned in exasperation. 'I am trying to do the honourable thing by giving you a choice here, you aggravating female. Go because you want to go or stay because you want to stay—no extra coercive strings attached, your damn choice!'

'Stay,' Lexi whispered.

He frowned again, as if she'd given the wrong answer. 'Why?' he charged. 'When I have given you nothing but aggravation, hassle and hurt?'

'I was just getting used to the idea of—of us trying to be married and…' She attempted a helpless little shrug within the firm grip of his hands. 'I still have feelings for you, OK?'

Defensive and tense, she waited for him to say something. He was still frowning down at her, but a searching glint was happening behind the frown, and at least that horrible blackness had left his eyes so she could see the golden bits again. The silence stretched. Lexi wished she knew what he was thinking. Like a stork, she swapped her weight from one leg to the other, then, because she couldn't stop it, she let out a soft, slightly husky, nervy little laugh.

'And I love your legs. You always did have great legs…'

'My legs?' Franco repeated.

Lexi nodded, biting down on the quiver moving across her lips. 'Kind of long, tough and tanned. Sexy—even with all the scars you've accumulated over—'

He shut her up with a hot, bruising kiss. She dropped the things she was holding because she needed to grab hold of his arms to steady herself. Somewhere in the back of her mind she knew they hadn't finished with the Claudia thing but did not want to think about that right now.

This was what mattered: the heat of his mouth claiming hers with the same burning hunger it used to, the remembered dark groan of pure pleasure when he felt her melting response. Franco had taught her everything she knew about the power of her own deep flowing rivers of passion and he plundered deep, savouring the eager heat with which she responded to him.

No drawing back this time. Lexi knew it as surely as she knew that Franco knew it. He meshed one of his hands into her hair, the other cupping the silk covered shape of her bottom to bring her close up against him so she could feel the power of his desire for her. Thick potent heat swam through her veins and pooled low between her thighs in an erotic swirl of excitement. Her hands moved, anxiously scoring over the soft cambric of his shirt and feeling the powerful set of his biceps, his shoulders, the alluring heat of him. Her bare legs made brushing contact with his, increasing the bright sting of need growing inside her as the hair-roughened quality of his skin rasped against her smooth softness. It was like being wired up to an electric grid and she quivered, her restless fingers clutching at him so tightly she felt him shudder, then flinch.

'Oh…' she choked, remembering, and drew her head back a little. Her heart was racing and she was breathing too fast. She clashed with the simmering darkness of his eyes. No gold in evidence—just dark, dark caverns of hunger she wanted to drown in. 'I hurt you,' she groaned.

'No,' he denied, and tried to recapture her lips, but Lexi held them away from him.

'I did,' she insisted. 'You're one big bruise, and I don't know how we are going to do this without putting you through torture.'

Franco released a short mocking laugh and moved his fingers against her bottom, sliding them sensually against silk as he eased her into greater contact with him. 'You think this isn't already torture?'

It was pure instinct that made Lexi move against his potent hardness, and he groaned and shuddered, his other hand shifting from her hair to her back, then sliding with a compulsive movement to her waist to press her even closer as he captured her mouth again and this time gave her no chance to think. Passion flared between them in a fevered hunger.

Liquid heat was pooling in just about every erogenous zone she possessed.

'I want you, *tesoro*, so badly it is eating away at me.' The heat of his lips moving across her cheek as he husked the words made her shiver as he tasted the sensitive flesh below her ear.

Lexi tilted her upper body back a little so she could begin unbuttoning his shirt. Her fingers trembled so badly she struggled over the simple task, and it didn't help that Franco was tasting her neck now, whispering words in low, sexy Italian while his hands dealt with the removal of her nightie in one smooth, deft move that sent the scrap of silk pooling to her feet.

Naked in front of him for the first time in years, she froze for a few seconds and he did the same thing, even taking a step back so he could look at her, the simmering flame of his study lashing her skin with hot stings which tightened the swelling tips of her breasts so her nipples bloomed like crowns of dusky pink. Reaching out, he cupped a hand around one breast—gently, as if he was reacquainting himself with its size and its weight. Seeing the power of his fierce concentration, Lexi stood perfectly still and watched him as he stretched out the other hand and curved it around the gentle swell of her hip.

The air around them throbbed with sexual tension. His shirt was hanging open, the wedge of dark hair trailing over his front to the waistband of his undershorts a virile contrast to the deep bronze sheen of his skin. Her tongue moistened in her mouth with a desire to lean in and taste him, her fingers twitching by her sides in an anxious need to move away the shirt. She could see the jutting evidence of his manhood pressing against his undershorts, traced its powerful length with her eyes. Memories of what it was like to feel him deep inside her awoke with an excitement that held her gripped in its thrall.

As if he could tell what she was thinking he moved his hand to her stomach, then stroked downwards—and she shivered out a gasp of expectancy just before his fingertips sank into the triangular cloud of dusky curls. As he made that first fingertip dip it was as if he was laying claim to something he believed was totally his. She was hot and she was damp and her body welcomed his touch by clenching the muscles there, which he felt with a brief, tense smile of acknowledgement.

By mutual need they came together again—urgent, maybe even a little desperate, their lips fusing while she dealt with the shirt, then moved to hook her fingers into the waist of his shorts. Pushing them down his lean, smooth, tautly muscled flanks, she felt his tremor and then his gasp as she stroked her fingers along his length, then closed them around him. His fingers became buried in her hair again, so he could tilt back her head. Her lips were already parted and ready to receive the driving force of his kiss that carried them all the way down onto the bed. Lexi found herself stretched out on the cool sheet and losing contact with him as Franco rid himself of his shorts.

When he stretched out beside her and then rolled onto her she saw his bruising. 'We should take this carefully,' she whispered worriedly.

'To hell with being careful,' he growled, then dipped his dark head and claimed a protruding nipple with the burning heat of his mouth. He grazed her with his lips, his teeth, the fiery heat of his breath as he slowly moved across the swollen mound of that breast to the other breast and captured the rosy peak with a searing hunger that dragged a keening cry from her lips.

'You taste like heaven,' he told her.

Her anxious fingers speared into the glossy thickness of his hair. 'Francesco...' was all she could manage to say in response.

'Si, amore, it is I.' He sounded amused, yet oddly sombre

at the same time. 'You remember this? How good we are together? How it took so little to drive us out of our minds?'

Each dark question was punctuated by a different caress
of his hands or his mouth. Lexi lay boneless and trembling
with the need for him to keep on touching her, writhing with
rising anxiety as he tracked kisses down her slender shape
to her waist then sank a deep-tongued caress into her navel,
where she'd always been way too sensitive to bear it without
turning into a wild thing.

He lifted his head to look at her, triumph pounding through
him at how thoroughly she'd lost control. He released a low
laugh and bent to issue the same torment again. Lexi caught
hold of the bulging muscles in his shoulders and sank her
nails in, squirming beneath him in an effort to get free from
such an overload of excruciating pleasure that was threatening to send her wild.

Then he wasn't laughing at anything. He was snaking back
up to claim her mouth in a deep, probing kiss. At the same
moment his fingers timed a controlled glide into the hot,
silken folds of her body. Lexi heard her heartbeat thunder-
ing in her ears and knew already she was careering close to
the edge of a climax the likes of which promised to knock
her off the planet with its intensity. Somewhere in the dim
background she could hear Franco trying to soothe her down
from the brink, but it wasn't going to happen. For more than
three years she had lived with all this passion crushed down
inside, so she would not have to feel its powerful pull ever
again. She'd let no other man get this close to her. She'd never
wanted to feel like this again—so helplessly out of control—
yet with this one particular man choice was lost to her.

She forgot about his injuries, his bruises, his wounded
thigh—everything, scoring his back and his chest with her
fingernails and moving her legs in quick, anxious need up
and down the corded muscles in his calves. She felt hot, breathless—totally governed by what she was feeling. 'Please,

Franco, please…' she heard herself begging, feverishly kissing his mouth, his jaw, his neck, dragging her hands down his body so she could close them once again around the velvet steel of his proud erection.

'Lexi…' he whispered unsteadily. 'Slow down, *amore.*'

But she didn't want to slow down. 'Please…' she gasped again. 'I missed you so much… Please, Franco, please…'

As she felt the tremors breaking over his long, powerful frame he surrendered to her pleas and with a groan slipped between her parted thighs, slid his hands beneath her, then let her guide him where she most needed to feel him before he smoothly, surely drove himself deep.

Exhilaration ran through him like the most potent pleasure drug ever invented as her muscles closed around him, eager, possessive. He pulsed. She clung and fused her mouth to his again. They lost themselves in a voyage of rediscovery—no holding back anything. When she tripped the wire of an electric orgasm it was too soon; but he revelled in each quivering shock wave, held on and held on, until he could do so no longer and finally released his own shattering shock waves of fulfilment while their mouths remained fused and the pounding of their hearts beat in unison.

It was like dying within the most exquisite pleasure ever and then waking up again later to find you'd discovered your soul mate. They lay in a tangle of boneless limbs, too shattered to be able to move. He was burning hot and heavy on her, but Lexi didn't mind. In fact she rejoiced in his weight, and his lingering pulse still beat a tantalisingly potent force inside her. She didn't want to think or even breathe if it meant spoiling this special moment. His head was pressed in against the curve of her neck and her shoulder. Her fingers held it there. She smiled dreamily, because she loved the feel of his tongue tasting the warm dampness of her skin there. *I feel whole again for the first time in years*, she thought dreamily.

'Lexi…'

'Hmm?' she mumbled.

'*Accidenti, cara*, but I cannot move.'

'Your bruises!' As if she'd been stung by a sharp implement, Lexi came alive with a jolt of her limbs that made Franco release a groan in protest. 'Didn't I say we should be more careful? Which bit hurts the most?'

He managed to lift his head up so he could look at her, a wry humour in his slumbrous dark eyes. 'All of me.'

'Shall I try squeezing out from beneath you?'

'I'm too heavy.'

'I know,' she teased, and he smiled a lazy smile.

Several minutes went by after that, because they ended up kissing, and the kisses were so gentle and tender there didn't seem any rush to figure out a way to separate themselves without hurting him.

'It is good to have you back where you belong, Signora Tolle,' Franco husked, tasting the corner of her mouth. 'Perhaps it is not a bad idea for us to remain like this for the rest of our lives.' He gave a tiny nudge with his hips to highlight his meaning. 'Someone will discover us in a few thousand years, still locked together like this turned to stone, and think we were so romantic.'

'I don't think Zeta will wait a few thousand years to check on us,' Lexi responded with a soft giggle.

In the end Lexi managed to slide out from beneath him, leaving Franco to collapse onto the bed.

'And to think I always considered you a really macho hunk.' Lexi sighed as she got up and started gathering their discarded clothes.

'I *am* a macho hunk,' he insisted, watching her move around the room. 'Did I not just perform with supreme macho efficiency even with cracked ribs and bruises?'

Lexi stopped what she was doing—perform with efficiency? Did he have to make it sound so—physical?

'When I think of all those months of marriage when we did not indulge in sex at all, it feels like a hell of a waste now.'

'Well, if you must think in those terms I suppose those months must have been a waste to you. But for me...' She started picking up clothes again—snatching them up, actually, because if she didn't she might— 'Talking like that makes me feel like just another sexual affair to you.'

An uneasy silence ensued for a few seconds before he said, 'I think you had better explain that.'

She turned to look at him lying there sprawled in all his naked glory like a beautifully tooled bronze sculpture even his bruising couldn't spoil. Arrogant, she thought. Conceitedly sure of his own masculine beauty. Even the sleepy weight of his eyelids and the kiss warmed shape of his mouth made statements of lazy self-assurance about the deeply sensual man that he was.

And why not? He'd sent her wildly out of control only two seconds after their skins met. When had she not responded like that?

'We had a fabulous summer affair and a lousy winter marriage.' She looked away again. 'One steaming hot—the other freezing cold. When I left here I don't think you even noticed.'

'I noticed,' he murmured.

'In passing? On your way back to your old life? Tell me.' Clutching the clothes to her front, Lexi made herself face him again. 'How long did you wait before you consoled yourself by taking another woman to your bed?'

His eyes hooded altogether. For a brief moment she thought she saw that grey veil attempt to shutter his grim face. 'I don't think this topic of conversation is appropriate.'

'Appropriate for what?'

'We are trying to heal the past.'

Well, Lexi didn't feel healed—she felt hurt. Wounded, in fact, by that shuttered expression. She wanted denials. Hot, offended denials. Not—

'Is this yet another subject on your banned list, Franco?' she goaded. 'Are we not to talk about the newspaper reports that put the first woman in your bed at the Lisbon powerboat convention a short month after I left?' She tugged in a short breath. 'Of course that was the first woman the press got wind of—that does not automatically mean she was the first one to grace your bed. Perhaps you had enough sensitivity to be more discreet about the preceding lovers—'

'And you moved straight in with Dayton,' he countered. 'You tell me, Lexi.' Despite the obvious aches of his body he climbed off the bed and moved towards her—prowled, actually, like a sleek hunter scenting a hearty meal he relished tearing to bits. 'How long did it take him to coax you into his bed? Did he use the *Let me hold you while you grieve for your baby* excuse to get you there? Did you curl up against him and weep your broken heart out all over him while he subtly moved things onto something much more satisfying and intimate?'

# CHAPTER NINE

GONE sickly pale now, she whispered, 'That's a disgusting thing to throw at me.'

'You think so?' Grim contempt scored lines across his handsome face. 'So did I when the bastard relayed those bald facts to me the day I was stupid enough to go to his apartment to see you.'

'That's a lie!' Lexi protested.

'Is it?' Reaching out, Franco yanked the clothes out of her nerveless fingers, separated his things, then stuffed her nightie back into her hands. 'Go to bed,' he snapped, and turned his back on her to head for the bathroom. 'Your own damn bed.'

But she couldn't move a single muscle. A cold, sickening chill of a tremor had frozen her where she stood. 'Bruce just would not lie like that... Why should he when it never happened?'

'That's right,' he derided. 'Trust loyal Bruce to always act in your best interests.' He stilled in the bathroom doorway. 'He showed me the evidence.'

'He what—?'

'He tried to fob me off with a verbal description first, then when I refused to accept it—' his big shoulders flexed in a ripple of tense glossy muscle '—he showed me the evidence.'

'But he can't have shown you any evidence when it didn't happen!'

The way she cried out that denial swung Franco round. His face looked as if it had been carved out of rock. 'Your things littered all over the place.' He speared a glance at the nightie she held crushed in her taut fingers. 'You always were the untidiest woman I ever met. When we lived our fantastic hot affair that summer you drove me crazy because you never picked up after yourself. On the boat. At the villa we rented in San Remo—'

San Remo...where everything had turned bad for them.

'He picked your bra up off the floor while I watched him,' he went on harshly. 'He dared...' In some distant part of her Lexi felt the emotional throb of his voice. 'He dared to send me a look, as if we were good old friends enjoying a moment of mutual understanding, as he tossed the damn bra onto a chair loaded down with your clothes.'

'This never happened.' Lexi took a step towards him, but he stiffened up so violently she pulled to a stop again.

'Don't tell me it didn't happen when I was there,' he ground out. 'I saw the damn frog sitting on your pillow!'

Lexi blinked in an effort to clear the glaze of confusion from her head. 'But—but that was m-my room.'

'With *his* stuff hanging in the wardrobes?'

'Yes!' she cried out. 'Bruce's clothes were in the wardrobes! You've seen him, Franco, you know what he's like about clothes! He—he must have a hundred Savile Row suits and two hundred shirts, and before I went to stay with him he spread them between the two bedrooms! I was only there for couple of months, so he didn't bother to clear them out!'

In the trammelling silence that followed her shrill explanation Lexi stared at Franco's angry face and took in the seething force of the vibrations still holding his naked frame so tense.

'Y-you came to see me—?' The frail shake wrapped around

that belated enquiry made him lower his eyelids over the turbulent shimmer in control of his eyes.

'A month after you left me.' He relayed that answer as if it had been dragged out of him by torture.

Lexi did not miss the significance of the month and the accusations she'd just thrown at him about his women. Clasping her arms around her body, she shivered.

'You were not there. He said you were attending several auditions in an attempt to get your stalled career back on track. He told me Hollywood beckoned,' he mocked bitterly, 'and you would be much better off if I...'

He didn't need to finish that sentence. Lexi found it too easy to finish it for herself. Bruce had tried to convince her to go straight back into acting, maintaining it would be the best way to work through her broken-hearted grief. He'd even set up auditions with a couple of famous directors that she'd refused to attend. When all attempts to make her see things his way had failed to move her, he'd offered her a job working with him at the agency instead.

And she'd accepted. Bruce had been determined to keep her close this time—no matter what it took. When she'd moved into her own flat he'd been angry for weeks...

'Oh, my God, he...' She flattened a hand against her mouth as the ugly words dried up like water droplets hitting a sand dune; but those watered grains of sand started melding together as everything about Bruce and their long relationship came together to make a sick kind of sense.

When Franco had accused Bruce of being a control freak he had not been plucking insults out of the air. He'd had hard evidence of exactly how much Bruce was trying to control her life. Then she remembered the other things Franco had called Bruce and nausea began to claw at her stomach. Unable to just stand there in the centre of the tumbling fallout happening inside her, Lexi turned in a dizzy reel to head for the bedroom door—only she couldn't make it that far, and ended up sinking weakly down on the side of the bed. For the last ten years Bruce had always been there, in the background of her life, a calm, often critical but always totally dependable figure watching over her—or waiting for her to grow up?

Then her mother had met Philippe and loosened the reins on her. Lexi had tripped off and fallen head over heels in love with her tall, dark, handsome Italian while all Bruce had been able to do was watch it happen and wait for the love affair to burn itself out—as, she supposed, everyone else had waited for it to burn out.

Still standing in the bathroom doorway, Franco was wishing he'd kept his damn mouth shut. He'd never meant to tell her any of that: now he'd brutally shattered her with it. And the way *he'd* regarded Dayton's obsession with Lexi did not necessarily mean it was as sinister as he'd made it out to be. Dayton was a good-looking guy, up there and out there, with a string of beautiful women trailing in and out of his life. The age gap between him and Lexi did not mean much in current society when, basically, if a guy still had it then he might as well go for it. His own father entertained liaisons with women with a wider age gap and no one batted a critical eye.

No, his view of Dayton was jaundiced by old-fashioned jealousy and the ten years the guy had hung on, waiting for Lexi to notice him as a prospective lover. He'd seen the desire in Dayton's face the first time he'd met him, known exactly where he was coming from, and had wanted to punch him ever since.

But none of that justified the way he'd made her face the truth about Dayton, because he'd done it to wound. Now he wanted to kick something because—damn it—how the hell was he going to tell her about Marco when he'd already wounded her enough with *this*?

Lexi didn't know he'd moved until she felt his fingers close around her wrists and she was pulled inexorably to her feet.

He wrapped her in his arms, the hairs on his chest tickling her nose as he heaved air into his lungs, then let it out again.

'I should not have said anything,' he said heavily. 'After the way we parted you had every right to try and put your life back together any way that you wanted to—'

'But wh—what you described never happened,' Lexi denied painfully.

'I know that now.' He drew her closer so her forehead rested against his chest.

Lexi tried to squeeze a hand between them so she could wipe a stray tear from her cheek. 'Why was everyone so against us, Franco?' she asked in a bewildered voice. 'What were we doing that was so terrible?'

His response rumbled against her brow in its gravity. 'They had their own agendas, Lexi. Dayton…Claudia…and…' Another sigh eased from him. 'What they wanted does not really matter to us—this matters.' Combing his fingers into her hair, he gently coaxed her to lift up her head. Their eyes met: his dark and somber, with bleak golden flashes; hers ocean pools of incomprehension and hurt. 'We are here, together, and we have not exactly hung around in making it back to this point. I call that fate giving them all a hard smack across the head for interfering in the first place.'

He wanted her to smile, to lighten the heavy weight in the atmosphere, but Lexi shook her head. 'It took a terrible accident and Marco's death to get us here,' she said sadly. 'Without the accident we would be talking through our lawyers about our divorce.'

'That's not true.' As she tried to pull away Franco tightened his arms around her. 'I told you I had already made up my mind I was coming to see you before the accident happened.'

'For what reason?' Her shrug told him she didn't understand why he should want to bother.

'Because I spent the last three years looking for a good excuse to do it.'

As she stilled in surprise at that dry confession, Franco lowered his head and kissed her soft, quivering mouth. Her lips clung—of course they did, she thought helplessly. He was just so gorgeously good at kissing.

'I missed you,' he said. 'I got on with my life, and the focus was probably good for business, but always in the background I missed you and what we had together. Can you tell me honestly that it was not the same for you?'

She couldn't deny it, but she was still too upset by what Bruce had done to do more than offer up a small shrug. Franco pulled her in close again and just held her. It was only when he felt her shiver he realised they'd been standing there stark naked while indulging in yet another argument.

'You're cold. Come on—let's go back to bed,' he decided.

'But you said—'

'I know what I said,' he interrupted. 'I have changed my mind.'

'I don't want—'

'I'm not offering.'

Taking hold of the fingers she still clutched around her nightie, he prised them open and took the scrappy garment from her, shook it out, then dropped it over her head. As the silk slid down over her body Lexi let him take her hand and lead her back to the bed. She curled up there and watched him. He dragged on his undershorts as if he was making big statements with the nightie and the shorts about what they were *not* going to do next.

Her eyes were glued to that potent part of him until it was covered up. She felt her heartbeat go haywire, that so familiar flicker of heat deep inside her flaring up.

'How are the bruises?' she asked a trifle breathlessly.

'Sore.' Reaching out to hit a switch that plunged them into

darkness, he came to lie down beside her. 'Next time show a little pity on me and do all the work.'

'You were so very good at it, though.' Lexi could not resist stroking her fingers down his chest as he dragged the sheets up over them, her senses indulging in a leap of excitement when he went still.

Supporting himself on one elbow, Franco looked down at her. Through the darkness her eyes sparkled up at him, and she was biting down into the cushion softness of her lower lip.

'You greedy minx,' he murmured accusingly.

Flushing, Lexi wriggled. 'Of course, if you're so sure you're not up to it...'

Without warning he rolled onto his back, catching hold of her to bring her to her knees beside him. Despite the sore bruises he still had more strength in his arms than Lexi gave him credit for.

'OK, *bella mia*,' he drawled. 'Take what you want. I am al! yours...'

Four days later, Lexi sat dangling her feet in the swimming pool and chewed pensively on her bottom lip as she watched Franco power his way up and down the length of the pool with the sun beating down on his glossy, wet bronzed back.

Tomorrow was Marco's funeral. For the last four glorious days they had not so much as touched on any subject likely to spoil the old harmony they'd resurrected that night in his bed—but it couldn't go on. She needed to shop for something suitably respectful to wear for the funeral, but the one time she'd asked if she could borrow a car to drive into Livorno he'd blocked the request with, 'You need anything, tell Zeta. She will get it for you.' Then he'd changed the subject.

His father was due home today. She'd heard Franco discuss his arrival over the telephone, using that same clipped blocking tone he'd used against her trip to the shops. In all the days she had been here he had not answered a single telephone call that had arrived in the house, leaving Zeta or Pietro to deal with whoever wanted to speak to him. He had, in effect, turned his home into a private sanctuary inside which the two of them lived as if the accident, or even the years they had been separated, had not taken place.

But his sanctuary was built inside a bubble that was about to burst, whether he wanted it to happen or not. He wasn't stupid, so whatever he was thinking behind the lazily relaxed mask of contentment he wore all the time Lexi knew he must be aware that he was going to have to burst this bubble soon.

'Franco…' she murmured as he swam up to the pool edge beside her legs.

'What?' he said, only to power away again. It was a very impressive demonstration of freestyle arrogance, because he'd been swimming up and down for fifteen minutes without stopping and did not look as if he was tiring yet. His bruises had already faded into the tanned lustre of his skin, and the wound on his thigh was nothing but a fine purple line to add to the others he already wore on his powerful legs. He would still wince occasionally if she accidentally put too much pressure on his ribcage, but other than that he was, she supposed, returned to full health—except for the blanket refusal to talk about Marco's death or his funeral.

As he powered back towards her Lexi timed the moment when she slid into the water and then stepped in front of him as he reached out to touch the pool edge. Finding the sun-kissed heat of her body obstructing him, he was quick to turn things to his advantage by taking hold of her waist and lifting her up as he rose like Neptune to his feet.

'Mmm, I've caught myself a real live mermaid,' he growled and tried to kiss her.

'That's corny.' Lexi frowned distractedly, tilting her head back out of his reach. 'We need to talk about—about tomorrow.'

'You like corny,' he insisted, and followed it up by capturing her mouth for a long, lazily sensual kiss. 'You like taking walks in the sultry moonlight and holding hands even when we are only walking downstairs—all corny, romantic stuff, *cara.*'

Refusing to be diverted, she insisted, 'We need to talk about tomorrow, Francesco.' She watched his expression change—tighten up—and, releasing a small sigh, cupped his damp face. 'Please listen to me,' she begged. 'You can't go on ignoring the fact that Marco will be laid to rest tomorrow, and that everyone you've been avoiding since the accident is going to be there.'

Frowning—no, scowling now, he countered very grimly, 'Yes, I can.'

'Well, I can't afford to ignore it, then.' Lexi changed tack. 'I need to buy something to wear for the funeral. I need to know how you want me to respond to questions about the two of us being together again.'

'You're not going.' Opening his arms, he dropped her back onto her feet.

'Yes, I *am*!' Lexi protested.

'You're staying here.'

He was about to dive back beneath the water again, but Lexi grabbed his arm to stop him. 'That is not your decision to make. Marco was my friend too, you know. I *liked* him!'

Shrugging her hand aside, he just turned and hit the water, then swam off! Bristling with frustration, Lexi heaved herself back out of the pool, grabbed a towel and wrapped it around her as she stalked off towards the house. Entering the back way, she headed grimly for the kitchens, found Pietro there enjoying a mid-morning snack, and asked if he would mind taking her into Livorno in half an hour.

Of course he couldn't say no to her, but she could tell by his wary expression as he agreed that he wished he could. It was the flickering way he glanced over her shoulder that made her realise why he was looking so wary. Franco stood a few feet behind her. As she spun around to look at him she caught the tail end of his frowning exchange with the other man.

Snapping her lips together, she pushed right past his obstructive frame and headed for the stairs. If he made it necessary she would call for a taxi to come and collect her, she decided stubbornly.

She'd pulled on a towelling robe and was scrambling through her small assortment of clothes looking for something to wear when she sensed Franco lounging in the bedroom doorway—the bedroom next door to the one they'd been sharing for the last four days.

'I'm not playing this game any more,' she announced without looking at him. 'I've let you get away with it for long enough.'

'I know.'

'You assured me days ago that you were not going to do something stupid, so you can quit with the blocking tactics— What do you mean, you know?'

Turning, she almost forgot how to breathe when she saw him standing there wearing nothing more than a pair of low riding swimming shorts and a towel hanging around his neck. He looked so much like the Franco from that long golden summer it came as a shock.

He shrugged a wide, still wet shoulder, the expression in his eyes shadowed by his spiky eyelashes. 'You cannot abide most of the people who will be there.'

'I am not paying my respects to *them*,' Lexi pointed out.

His small sigh accepted that. 'I predict it will be more like a circus than a funeral—the press will be crawling around all over the place, and you would have to be nice to Claudia.'

'I can do nice when I know I need to,' Lexi said stiffly, interpreting from his words that he didn't want her to go to Marco's funeral because he was afraid she would get into an unseemly cat fight with Claudia. 'I played nice with Claudia

when she was here weeping all over you. I can also appreciate that she has just lost her brother. You forget—I've been
there. I lost my mother not so long ago. I remember how bad
it feels to lose someone you love.'

'OK…' He moved, taking the towel from around his neck
to use it to rub his wet hair. 'I don't want you there.'

Hurt beyond bearing by that blunt announcement, Lexi
felt herself go pale. 'Are you ashamed of me or something?'

He should have come back with a quick, explosive *no*,
but he did not answer, and his silence was like a stiletto sliding smoothly into her chest. Lexi turned back to the clothes
closet and blindly selected something to wear with fingers
that shook so badly she dropped the skirt she'd slid from its
hanger and had to bend to pick it up.

'It is not a case of being ashamed, Lexi,' he sighed out suddenly. 'I just want to protect you from any cruel gossip that
might blow up.'

But he'd spoken too late, and his explanation did not make
any sense—unless…

'Gossip about you and your other women, by any chance?
Well, since you put that subject on the banned list, along with
just about everything and everyone else, let me inform you
that I have an imagination, Franco. I've already worked out
that more than half the women there will probably know you
as intimately as I do—including Claudia!'

'Damn it,' he said again. 'That is not what I meant!'

'Well, try speaking in straightforward sentences!' she
launched at him. 'Because all you've done since I came back
to Italy is toss out these cryptic messages to me, so how am I
supposed to know what you mean? Oh, although I *do* recall
you being very eloquent about my relationship with Bruce!'

'Don't bring *him* back into this,' Franco growled irritably.
'I have something I need to tell you, but I've been trying hard
to hang on until after the funeral. The thing is, I cannot be

sure how many other people know, so I would rather not put you in the firing line for a bloody great shock.'

'Then get it over with and tell me now.'

'No,' he muttered.

'Why?' she persisted.

'Because I want to damn well wait!' He lost his rag so spectacularly he made Lexi blink at him. *'Santa cielo,'* he rasped, throwing his hands up, 'can I not be allowed to get through the next twenty-four hours without all this aggrava-tion from you? Why can't you just trust that I know what I am doing? Is it too much to expect plain and simple support from you for one more day?'

He was talking about Marco. It finally registered with Lexi that he'd been engaging his blocking tactics since she'd ar-rived here in Italy because the 'something' he was keeping from her involved his closest friend. Now the grey pallor was definitely back, she saw, and the strain was dragging on his features, almost painful to see.

'OK,' she whispered. 'I won't ask again until you're ready to tell me.'

For some reason her promise did not seem to make him any happier. 'You can come to the funeral if that's what you want to do. But I tell you this, Lexi: move one half-inch away from my side and I will do something we both regret—got that?'

Wanting to ask why he had changed his mind, Lexi gauged the sizzling tension emitting from him, pressed her lips to-gether and just nodded her head.

He moved back to the door with the grim stride of a man glad to leave the room. An hour later a car arrived to deliver a selection of outfits suitable to wear at a funeral for Lexi to choose from.

Franco had shut himself away in his study and she did not see him again for the rest of the day. It felt as if she was being punished for standing up to him and spoiling their few days of harmony. By the time they met up again for dinner his father had arrived home, and their meal was a very stressful, sober affair, with the prospect of what was to take place the next day hanging heavily over all three of them.

The two men excused themselves from the table as soon as the meal was over. They disappeared into the study—to talk business, Lexi presumed—and in a lot of ways she was glad they'd left her alone. Franco might be talking to his father again; but throughout dinner his tone had been flat and stilted and Salvatore was either too jet-lagged to bother taking on his son in the mood he was in, or he was as aware as Lexi that Franco was treading a very fine line emotionally.

That night she slept in her own bed. She wasn't sure why she made the decision to do that, but when Franco made no effort to come and find her she assumed that he was glad she'd given him the space to be on his own.

Not that it lasted. Halfway through the long, empty night she'd spent lying wide awake, worrying about him because he'd become so distant and withdrawn, she gave in to the craving that had been eating away at her since she'd heard his bedroom door close hours ago and got up, sneaked into the darkness of his room, then slid into the bed beside him.

He was awake. It didn't surprise her.

'Shh,' she whispered before he could say anything. 'You don't need to talk. I just needed to hold you.'

And he let her. He took her advice and said not a word, but at least he curved an arm around her to draw against him. They stayed like that for what was left of the night, paying silent vigil to the ordeal to come.

## CHAPTER TEN

THEY came to mourn Marco in droves. Masses of people packed the church, spilling onto the grounds and onto the street. He was well known and well liked, and the tragedy of his young age and his spectacular death made the mourning of Marco all the more poignant.

Lexi stood quietly beside Franco. His father flanked his other side. Behind them stood the full *White Streak* team, although in their sober black suits, Lexi had not recognised them until they'd lined up outside the church, waiting in turn to commiserate with Franco over Marco's loss. Each one of them had cast a curious glance at Lexi before moving respectfully away.

In front of them stood the Clemente family. Marco's mother and father, his sister Claudia and his many other relatives, all grief-stricken and bereft, but still eager to commiserate with Franco over the loss of his lifelong friend. When they'd arrived inside the church Marco's *mamma* had thrown herself against Franco's chest to sob her heart out. He'd held her close and murmured soothing words to her that had thickened his voice and driven the colour from his face. They'd all asked concernedly how Franco was doing. His stilted dismissal of his own injuries made it clear to Lexi that he found his situation in all of this almost too hard to bear.

She began to appreciate why he had locked himself away

from it all. Survivor guilt, she thought, listening to his quiet voice making sombre responses and feeling his tension like a swarm of stinging bees attaching themselves to her flesh. She knew that he did not want people's sympathy and commiserations, though he had to accept them. And as the ordeal lengthened through the Catholic Mass she could feel the stinging buzz of Franco's tension increasing, until she worried he might actually turn and make a bolt for it.

What he did do almost snapped the fine thread of her own self-control.

It was Marco's father who turned to him and gravely invited him to say a few words for their son. Franco must have been expecting it to happen, because he stepped out from their pew and onto the podium with no hint of hesitation—yet she'd felt the fine tremor rip through him a second before he'd moved. He spoke with a quiet, grave fluency about his friendship with Marco, spanning its twenty years with precious memories, causing a fresh wave of aching grief to spread through the gathered assembly. Even Salvatore became overwhelmed.

Had Franco been composing all this while he lay awake last night? Was this the reason he had shut himself away in his study for half the day?

Lexi felt a sinking twist of guilt: she had not appreciated what he must have been struggling with while she'd fought with him yesterday. He had not wanted her to come. He'd wanted to get through the day without the need to worry about her and the curiosity he knew her presence beside him would evoke. He'd tried to block out all reference to Marco since the accident—yet here he stood, having to open up his grief and loss in front of hundreds of people. She hurt for him—hurt so badly she reached out and clung to Salvatore's hand. She fought back her own rush of tears—for Marco and for Franco.

From the church they moved in sombre procession to

Marco's final resting place, and still the day did not end there. Next they drove to the Clemente estate, with its world-famous vineyards and beautiful *cascina*.

'OK?' she dared to whisper to Franco as the three of them sat in the rear of Salvatore's Mercedes.

'*Si,*' he responded, but that was all he said.

'You did well, Francesco,' Salvatore said huskily. 'I am proud of you today.'

This time Franco did not make an answer—for what could he say? This was still not over. They had a wake to attend, time to relax a little and socialise; but all he wanted to do was tell Pietro to turn the car around and take them home.

He got through the first hour by choosing to avoid those people who knew Lexi from their summer together. They were all there—the golden people, as she'd used to call them, most of them friends of his still. People who seemed, thankfully, to want to respect the politics of reverence and politeness by keeping their distance. Though he could see they were curious to see Lexi with him—and perhaps a little uncomfortable too, for none of them had treated her particularly well.

Even Claudia kept away from them, which he found coldly amusing. She must have worked out by now that Lexi would have told him the part she'd played in breaking them up. They ate delicate finger food from platters extended to them by circulating waiters, talked when they needed to, and then, quite suddenly, it all became too much for him. He was standing with Lexi by his side, talking to a lawyer friend, when it happened. From the corner of his eye he saw Claudia making her way towards them, and he knew he could not be pleasant to her—no matter how much today was about putting personal grievances aside. Abruptly excusing them, he grabbed Lexi's hand and walked her out through the French windows and along the terrace until they'd put the majority of the people at a distance.

He didn't know why it was happening but he felt so hot, and his heart was pounding. Leaning a shoulder against one the stone pillars that supported the loggia, he let go of Lexi's hand so he could loosen his tie and drag open a couple of buttons on his shirt, then he breathed in a lungful of humid air.

'Are you all right?' Looking up at his face, Lexi felt concern clutch at her stomach because he looked as if he might just pass out.

'Fine,' he said. 'Just hot and…'

Reaching up, she touched he hand to his pale cheek. 'You don't feel hot. You feel quite cool.'

'Inside hot,' he enlightened her. 'How much longer do you think we have to stay?'

He was asking *her* that question? Lexi lowered her hand and looked out across the garden to where the Clemente vines marched in regimented lines towards the horizon.

Throughout the whole long day he had barely spoken to her. He'd kind of worn her like a side arm, kept tucked in close to him and hidden almost out of sight. If it had not been for the way he'd tightened his grip if she so much as tried to move away from him she would have thought he'd forgotten she was even there. Twice she'd actually got away from him. Once to say a private farewell to Marco before they'd left his flower bedecked graveside, and the other time when they'd first arrived here and she'd made a quick visit to the cloakroom. When she'd turned away from Marco's grave Franco had been standing just a few yards away waiting for her to go to him. The next time he'd been waiting for her right outside the cloakroom door. Both times he'd said nothing, his expression as impenetrable as the self-control he'd been exerting. He'd just caught her hand and drawn her back to his side, then returned them to the throng.

It was an absolute no-brainer that he'd meant what he'd said about her not straying from his side. It was also a no-brainer that he had no intention of allowing her the chance to talk to anyone on her own.

'You're the boss,' she therefore responded, a trifle satirically. 'I'm just your mute sidekick.'

He melted her bones with a slow grin. 'You are the bossy one in this partnership,' he threw at her lazily. 'You threw my friends off my boat when you'd had enough of them. You dragged me out of clubs and restaurants without bothering to ask me if I was ready to leave. You even flirted with any man in your vicinity then told me off if I dared to complain.'

Flushing when she realised he was only telling it as it had been back in that golden summer, Lexi grimaced. 'It's no wonder your friends didn't like me much.'

'That's a joke.' He laughed. 'The guys, at least, were fascinated by you and jealous of me. They used to wish it was them you were dragging away.'

Lexi looked at the stone floor beneath her shoes. 'I didn't want *them* to myself.'

'I know,' Franco murmured.

'And if I was bossy with you, I don't recall you putting up much resistance.'

'That is because I didn't want to resist,' he told her dryly. 'I like it that you made all the decisions and trailed me around like your sidekick, *bella mia*.'

He was just teasing her when he said that, Lexi decided, and responded with a rueful smile. 'So today you're getting your own back on me?'

Said lightly as a tease-back, she did not expect all hint of humour to suddenly drain away from him. 'No, today is about respecting Marco's death and getting through this without—' He stopped, swallowed, then made a gesture with one of his hands before deciding roughly, 'Let's get out of here.'

Giving her barely a chance to register his meaning, he was grabbing hold of her hand and pulling her further along the terrace, so fast she had a struggle to keep up with him.

'But where are we going?' she demanded breathlessly.

'Around the house to the front. Pietro will take us home.'

'But we can't just leave without telling anyone! It would be rude—and what about your father? Franco!' She sighed when he just kept on going. 'Will you just stop and listen to me?'

But he didn't stop and listen. Within minutes they were in the back of his father's Mercedes and driving away from the Clemente estate, with a bewildered Pietro at the wheel.

'Pietro will come back for my father,' he said, before Lexi could repeat the question. 'We are only half an hour away.'

'But…you just walked out on Marco's wake,' she gasped, because she was still struggling to believe he had done it.

He made no comment, and if Lexi had believed he could block out everything he didn't want to talk about before this moment, she soon learned during the half-hour drive back to Monfalcone that he could put up a solid brick wall against any argument she attempted to make.

He didn't speak a single word. He just sat there beside her, pale and still, with a brooding frown strapped to his face. His mood disturbed her—it was disturbing Pietro too, because she kept seeing him taking quick frowning glances at Franco through the rearview mirror as he drove.

The car came to a stop at the front doors and then he was climbing out and coming round to open her door for her, placing a hand on her arm to help her out.

'OK, this is what's going to happen.' He spoke at last as they walked into the house to the sound of Pietro taking off back to the Clemente estate to collect Salvatore. 'You are going to pack a bag—casual things—while I find Zeta. I will see you back here in fifteen minutes.'

'But—where am I going now?' Lexi cried out as he strode off towards the kitchens.

'We are going away for a few days,' he said. 'Fifteen minutes, Lexi, or you come as you are!'

Staring after him, Lexi worried that the day been just too much for him to deal with. Had he flipped again? Was that it? Cursing herself for forgetting that only a week ago Dr Cavelli had been warning her of his concerns about Franco's mental health, she was seriously considering ringing the hospital to ask the doctor's advice when Franco came striding back, to find her still standing in the hall, as pale a ghost and as anxious as hell.

He must have known what she was thinking because he pulled to a stop, letting out a sigh. But all he said was, 'You have decided to come with me as you are?'

It was a challenge and a smoothly delivered threat at the same time. And, strangely, there was something about him— the way he looked and the way he was moving—that told her this was the real Franco, the cool, decisive one who thought on his feet and did not waste time explaining himself. He wasn't crazy—just determined.

'If I come with you, you'd better not be losing your mind again, because I won't like it!' she launched at him stressfully.

'I am not crazy,' he delivered incisively. 'Are you coming?'

'Of course I'm coming.' She made a dash for the stairs.

'Ten minutes, Lexi,' he called after her.

'Damn you, Franco,' she snapped right back.

But she still arrived back in the hall within the ten minutes, wearing jeans and sandals, her weekend bag hastily packed, to find that he had changed into similar clothes and was already waiting for her. A set of car keys jangled impatiently in his hand and a bag sat on the floor beside him along with a soft-sided cool bag. The moment Lexi arrived at his side he picked the bags up and walked outside.

She stepped outside and saw his red Ferrari glinting in the sunlight and she knew they were about to indulge in yet another spat.

'You're not allowed to drive for another week,' she said. 'It's on the "dos and don'ts" list the hospital sent home with you!'

Simmering in silence at the rebuke, he just tossed her the car keys, removed her bag from her grasp, then strode off to put the bags in the boot.

He had to be really eager to leave here, Lexi thought nervously. Trembling now—she had not expected this response from him—Lexi could only stare as he opened the passenger door and climbed into the car. His quickly changing moods were beginning to get to her, and on top of that she had never, *ever*, driven a car like this one.

Sucking in a deep breath, she got in behind the wheel.

Next he tossed a pair of sunglasses at her. They wanted to fall off her nose, because the frames were too big, but she didn't dare say anything because she knew why he had done it. He wanted her to protect her eyes from the flickering sun between the trees when she drove down the lane.

He had to instruct her as to how she moved the seat forward, and even how to start the great beast of a thing. Moving off as if she was driving an army tank, she was surprised to discover the controls were actually quite sweet. As they passed the place where she'd ditched her own car three and a half years ago anyone could have plucked tunes on the tension between them.

'Now you are back, I'm will have a hedge laid in those gaps,' he muttered. 'And the next car I buy you will be a bloody great land cruiser, not some flimsy cute baby sedan.'

She dared to glance at him and saw that he was pale. 'I didn't lose the baby because I crashed into a ditch, you know,' she told him gently.

'We will never know that for sure.'

'Yes, we do,' she insisted. 'I lost the baby because there had been a problem with the placenta. It happens, *caro*...'

The *caro* brought his face round. It was the first time she'd used the endearment, and his darkened eyes held onto hers so intensely she had to ease her foot down on the brake to slow them right down or risk another accident.

'We still get the hedge,' he husked—and it was really a very silly conversation, because right at that moment neither of them was thinking about hedges or the size of a car or even her doomed pregnancy.

Dragging her eyes free from his, she concentrated on the road ahead again, wondering if sexual tension could be bad for you—because she was feeling decidedly light-headed right now.

Lexi negotiated the narrow bridge with care, a troubled frown creasing her smooth brow. 'You keep talking about us as if we're really back together, but that's not what I agreed to,' she reminded him, pleased with herself that she hadn't scraped the car's shiny red paint.

'So I am still on trial? Is that what you're saying?'

Was she? Lexi thought about that for a minute. 'Our marriage is on trial,' she revised. It had to be—at least until she knew what that 'something' he was still holding back from telling her was.

They reached the junction that met with the main highway. 'Which way?' she asked.

'We go to Livorno.'

'To your apartment?'

'We are going to the Tolle docks,' he enlightened her.

As if he'd lit the litmus on her self-control, Lexi exploded. 'We are not going anywhere near the wreck of your bloody stupid powerboat, Francesco!'

'When did I say that I wanted to check out the *White Streak*?' he demanded in bewilderment.

That was the trouble. He didn't tell her anything, so she had to guess what he was thinking! 'Then why are we going to the Tolle docks?'

'Because,' he said, 'the *Miranda* is there.'

'You still have the *Miranda*?'

'All shipshape and ready to sail.' He nodded. 'We are taking her out. Give me a shout when you need directions,' he said, then stretched himself out in the seat and closed his eyes!

Lexi bit down on her tongue to stop herself from demanding to know who he thought he was, casually making that decision without any input from her. But then he'd been making decisions all over the place without bothering to request any input from her.

And he called *me* bossy, she thought, turning them onto the main highway. Then she tracked back, and felt a happy little fizz of excitement erupt deep down. The *Miranda*. She'd fallen in love with his boat from the very first day he'd taken her out on it. They'd spent the best times of their summer together on the *Miranda*, sailing along the French and Italian Riviera in a flotilla of sailing yachts, keeping his friends close but not so close they could intrude on what the two of them had going on.

'I thought you would have built yourself a newer, more up-to-date yacht by now,' she murmured.

'I have,' he confirmed, without opening his eyes. 'But the *Miranda* is—special.'

Because the yacht held special memories for him too?

As she drove them on towards Livorno Lexi saw herself as she'd looked the first time he'd invited her to spend the day with him on the *Miranda*. She'd worn a little red bikini with a skimpy red sarong around her waist. Franco had had on his usual shorts and a T-shirt, and she'd smiled at him but felt so shy she hadn't been able to look into his eyes. The thrill of being alone with him for the first time had charged up her senses, and she'd felt quivery on the inside, breathless and flushed.

'Thanks,' she'd mumbled, landing lightly by his side in rubber-soled flip-flops. It was the first time she'd noticed how he towered over her—big and dark and potently sexy. 'Wh—where can I stash this?'

The brightly coloured canvas bag that swung from one of her sun-kissed shoulders had contained everything she'd considered she might need for a day's sailing.

'I will do it.' Smooth as anything, he'd lifted the bag from her shoulder and carried it over to the sleek, low bulkhead that gave access to whatever was below decks. She'd tried to take a peek, but he'd blocked her view as he'd come back up on top, forcing her to take a couple of hurried steps back.

'You're skittish,' he'd said, and started frowning. 'You are not scared of me are you?'

'Of course I'm not,' she'd answered firmly.

He'd pointed towards the cream leather seating that hugged the shallow basin in which they stood. 'Then sit down and relax.'

She remembered sitting down and thinking, *Claudia Clemente is going to kill me when she finds out about this.* She'd known even then that Claudia wanted Franco all to herself, Lexi recalled, frowning as she steered the car onto the street leading down to the Tolle docks. Back then, though, she had not understood the kind of enemy she was making for herself. So she'd gone out for a day's sailing with Francesco Tolle and become his lover before they'd sailed back into Cannes.

'A fast mover,' she murmured now.

*'Scuzi?'* the man lazing beside her responded.

'You,' Lexi enlightened him. 'For our first date you took me out sailing for the day, but I don't remember that we did much sailing. You had me below decks and spread out on your bed before I'd managed to draw in more than a couple of breaths.'

'Two hours twenty minutes. I was counting… Pull in at the gates just ahead,' he instructed and sat up. 'I thought I was very patient.'

'With a bet on the table I suppose you *would* think like that.'

'Lexi, you know I did not make love to you because of some stupid bet,' Franco sighed out irritably.

Did she know that? Yes, she knew that. Somehow the bet was losing its importance. Lexi frowned when she made that discovery.

She pulled in at the gates as instructed, and a security guard came out of his office, touching his brow to acknowledge Franco, grinning at Lexi because she was in charge of his flashy red super car. He opened the gates.

'This place is vast,' she said, sitting forward so she could look curiously around her. She had never been here before, and she kept twisting her neck to the left and the right in an effort to take in the huge buildings on either side of them as she drove. 'Do you ever get lost in here?'

'Never,' drawled the man, with insufferable self-confidence. 'Take the next left. It leads to my private marina.'

His 'private marina'? It made Lexi pull a face. 'Where are your offices?'

There was a pause before he answered, and when he did speak his voice was as dry as dust. 'Three miles in the other direction, *cara*. You don't have a clue what kind of family you married into, do you?'

'You build big ships,' Lexi informed him.

'Ah, *si*.' Franco mocked that simplistic response. 'We even build little ones occasionally—and there she is…'

And there she truly was…

Staring through the windscreen at the sleek white-painted yacht glistening in the sunshine, Lexi felt a lump of helpless tears grow thick in her throat. There were other boats moored in the marina, a couple of them very impressive-looking; but Lexi only had eyes for the *Miranda*.

'She still looks so pretty,' she whispered softly. Not too big, not too small, but just—perfect.

It was like bumping in to a long lost friend when you least

expected it, and she laughed as she brought the car to a stop beside the aft deck and climbed out. She didn't think twice about stepping from the quay onto the *Miranda*, and then just stand looking around her.

In the process of collecting their things from the boot of the car, Franco viewed the smile that had softened her face. So she still had good memories about the *Miranda*, he thought—and hoped he was not about to ruin them.

'Here,' he said, swinging their bags one by one towards her so she could catch them and place them on the deck before he joined her. He handed her the cool bag. 'You stash this stuff in the galley while I see to these.'

He strode ahead with the other bags, leaving Lexi to follow him down the narrow steps that led below. Nothing had changed down here. The same wood still covered most surfaces, and the same smell of fresh varnish caught her nose. A table that doubled as a bed when needed took up most of the cramped space next to the tiny galley kitchen, and the same nautical maps still decorated the walls. As Franco strode towards the other end of the boat Lexi lifted the cool bag onto the narrow work surface in the galley, then bent to open the fridge door.

'I'll go and start the engine,' Franco said as he passed by her again. 'Join me on deck when you've finished down here.'

He disappeared, leaving her staring into the small fridge, surprised to find it was already chilled and that someone had stocked it with basic provisions. He must have planned this trip before they'd even left the house this morning, she realised, frowning as she added the plastic cartons of meals prepared by Zeta into the crowded fridge.

The engine fired and she rushed to finish what she was doing, then clambered back on deck. Franco was standing by the wheel, his head tilted to one side, listening with expert ears to the engine's quiet purr.

'Someone's been in and stocked the fridge,' she relayed. 'How long have you been planning this trip?'

'Come and take the wheel while I cast off.'

Once again he walked away without answering her question. Irritation snapping at her, Lexi took hold of the cool aluminium wheel and watched him pull in the ropes, using a foot to shove them off from the quay. She felt the *Miranda*'s smooth gliding movement and tightened her grip on the wheel.

'OK, ease out the throttle,' Franco instructed.

'No,' she refused. 'You come back here and do it. I haven't been near a boat since the last time I was on this one. I've forgotten what to do!'

'No, you have not.' He came to stand right behind her. 'Just look straight ahead and go easy on the throttle… Your "dos and don'ts" rulebook says I am not allowed to do it, Lexi,' he informed her coolly.

'Oh…' Crestfallen by the unwelcome reminder, she asked, 'Does the same rule count on the sea?'

'No idea.' He didn't sound as if he cared, either. 'However, since you brought up the rule thing you now have to deal with it. So take us out of here so we can catch some breeze and put up the sail.'

There was no arguing with that kind of logic. Lexi felt hoist by her own petard. Crushing her bottom lip between her teeth, she clutched at the wheel with one hand and reached out to clasp the throttle stick with the other. A tiny fizz of alarm churned her insides as the engine took hold and the yacht powered forward.

Tossing back her hair to send it streaming over her shoulders, Lexi concentrated so hard on steering them towards the gap between the two breakwaters that her eyes began to sting; but she didn't care. She'd forgotten how long the *Miranda* was, how sensitive she was to the smallest movement of the wheel.

'Don't you dare move away from me,' she warned tensely.

'I'm right here.' He rested his hand on her waist in reassurance. 'Take us out onto the open sea, *cara*. Enjoy yourself,' he encouraged softly.

Franco was glad she could not see the bleakness on his face right now. For this was it. He had kept his silence for long enough, and as soon as he found a place they could safely anchor, where she couldn't jump ship, he was going to tell her everything he had been holding back. He'd held true to the Italian belief that you did not speak ill of the dead before they had been laid to rest. He'd done it in respect for his long friendship with Marco, and because he'd needed the extra time with Lexi to bring her to the point where she was beginning to believe in them again.

'We're coming up to the breakwaters,' she whispered, as if this was the beginning of a fabulous adventure.

Detecting her small tremor of excitement, Franco eased closer to the warmth of her body. 'Steady as she goes, *cara*,' he intoned gently. 'Be ready to feel the difference between the calm water inside the marina and the first tug of the ocean swell.'

'Which way when we get there?'

'I don't have a clue.'

He sounded as if he didn't care. 'So we're just sailing off into the sunset? Running away like we ran away from Marco's funeral?'

'Concentrate on what you are doing,' was all he said.

'Why are you constantly stonewalling me when I ask you something?' Lexi snapped out in frustration. 'You never used to be like this. You used to be a really open guy I could talk to!'

'I am still quite desperately in love with you. Is that open enough for you?'

Lexi almost swerved them into the solid mass of the breakwater, forcing Franco to place his hands over hers on the wheel to guide the *Miranda* back onto a safe course, while she just stood with his smooth declaration playing in her head and rolling her emotions up in a ball that stuck hard in her throat.

Franco sensed the clamour inside her. He felt the tremor of her hands beneath the steadying grip of his on the wheel. The swell hit them portside. He took control of the throttle with Lexi trapped between him and the wheel, a useless player, while his sailing head took over and he guided them onto a smoother course. The wind caught her hair and blew it back across his shoulders. He glanced down and caught a glimpse of her face turned pearlescent pale.

'No comment?' he drawled in wry observation. 'The lady has finally stopped talking.'

'Your timing is useless.' Lexi burst into shrill trembling speech. 'I could have killed us just then!'

'I am good at driving people to kill.'

That flat comment hit her like a punch in the stomach. Lexi groaned and spun around to look up at him. 'You didn't kill Marco,' she told him painfully.

'You think not?' Still in control of the *Miranda*, he flicked her a brief cynical glance. 'You were not there. You don't know what happened.'

'It was an accident,' Lexi insisted. 'You hit turbulence and…'

'Time to put up the sails.'

'Stop doing that!' Sheer frustration made her hit out at him, her clenched fist making contact with his rock-solid chest. He winced. She quivered in remorse when she realised where she'd hit him. 'Sorry.' She smoothed the flat of her hand over the area she'd just punched. 'But you have just got to stop shutting me out!'

'I know,' he sighed after a minute. 'I just want you to know where I'm coming from before I stop shutting you out.'

Standing taut within the circle of his arms, she asked, 'What is it that you're finding so hard to tell me, Franco, that can be worse than what we've already said to each other?'

He looked down, his eyes narrowed against the glint of the sun on the water. She felt his chest heave up and down beneath her resting palms. He parted his lips to let the air out, then looked back at the shimmering horizon ahead of them with the stunning Italian coastline sliding by them on one side.

'I think Marco meant to kill himself,' he said, then swallowed thickly and brought his teeth together in a tense clench.

Too shocked to respond, Lexi froze for a few seconds, then, 'No,' she said thickly. 'Please don't say things like that.'

'Or maybe he meant to kill me and made a damn mess of it—' This time a tense laugh raked the back of his throat.

'For goodness' sake, Franco—why would you suspect something like that?' she demanded painfully. 'He was your friend!'

'No, he wasn't. Look...' he sighed again. 'Can we finish this later? I need to find a place we can anchor or risk sending us the same way that Marco went...'

This time he wasn't trying to block her out, Lexi realised; she could hear the difference in his voice. And his face wasn't wearing that awful grey cast, nor his eyes that black blank look. He was genuinely struggling to concentrate.

'Do you want me to put the sail up?' she offered, earning herself a tense twitch of a smile.

'What I want is for you to be gloriously impulsive like you used to be and grab me and kiss me then tell me how much you love me. But I don't suppose—'

'All right. I love you, OK?' Lexi complied swiftly. 'Just stop th—thinking such horrible thoughts.'

'You're going to take that back later,' he predicted.

'No, I won't—not unless I'm the crazy one around here,' she responded candidly. 'Because I can't think of one other reason for letting you put me through this last week. I must still love you.'

'Gagged by the doctor, chained to my bed, beautifully manipulated by my father to make you stay with me.' Franco listed the measures he had taken to keep her with him. 'Now I have trapped you on the *Miranda* in the middle of the ocean so you can't run away.'

'Thanks for the excuses,' Lexi murmured tautly. 'Shall I do the sail now?'

Franco shook his head. 'We don't need it. I've spotted somewhere to anchor.'

As he turned the boat towards land Lexi spun in the circle of his arms and saw the heat misted cliffs soaring up in front of them: a spectacular sight. The colour of the ocean darkened to deep green as they sailed into a tiny cove cut out from the rockface. Franco cut the engine, then instructed her to take the wheel while he headed aft to let down the anchor.

Silence suddenly engulfed everything. The *Miranda* swayed gently beneath her feet. She watched Franco walk towards her, then come to a stop, and even with the sun beating hotly down on her Lexi felt a chill cover her flesh when she looked into his face.

'OK, here it is.' He was not going to hang around with this now. 'Marco stopped being my friend in San Remo, when he told me he'd slept with you the night I had to leave you alone to deal with some business for my father in Milan.'

# CHAPTER ELEVEN

FRANCO watched Lexi's face and saw exactly what he had expected to see. First came the confused frown, then the dawning shock of utter disbelief. Then came the question—he was waiting for the question.

'You believed him?'

*'Si,'* he confirmed.

'But—why?' she breathed in bewilderment.

'He was very convincing.'

'And the closest thing you had to a brother,' Lexi offered thickly. 'While I was just your summer distraction who stupidly got pregnant?'

'He told me this before you found out you were pregnant.'

Lexi dipped her head and closed her eyes, reliving the way Franco had gone cold towards her. She felt the pangs of her own hurt all over again, because she'd believed that he'd become bored with her as his friends had told her he would. Then Claudia had sent her proof of the bet and within twenty-four hours her mother had died, sending her life into free-fall. Quite pathetically, she recognised now, she'd turned to Franco for support and he'd let her. He'd supported her right through the coming weeks while she buried her mother and learned that Philippe had spent her money. Then to top it all off she'd realised she was—

She pulled in a deep, painful breath. 'You thought the baby was Marco's.'

Franco ran a set of tense fingers through his hair. 'I thought it could be possible,' he admitted. 'I'd always been so careful with you, so it made sense.'

'Did you tell him what you suspected?'

'No,' he answered.

'Why not?' Lexi demanded. 'If you believed I'd been to bed with him, was carrying his child, why didn't you tell him? Why take responsibility for me onto yourself?'

'You needed me, not him—'

'Oh, well, thanks for being so noble, Franco! Thanks for marrying me and turning the next four months into the worst days of my life!'

He couldn't argue with that. He *had* married her and made her a life a misery. He'd made his own life a misery. He hadn't wanted to be near her but he hadn't wanted any other man near her either—especially not Marco.

'I was in love with you.'

'Oh, don't feed me that old chestnut,' Lexi condemned in trembling disgust. 'I was the bet you all wanted to win that summer—the jolly joke you all had at my expense!'

'It started out like that.' He finally admitted it. 'But that lasted only as long as it took me to get to know you.'

'Bed me, you mean.'

'No,' he denied.

'Yes!' Lexi insisted, throwing herself past the wheel and down into the galley because she had a horrible fear she was going to be sick. She heard Franco follow her down there. 'I don't know how you managed to live with yourself afterwards,' she tossed at him angrily as she bent to grab a bottle of water out from the fridge. And she was trembling, white as a sheet and hating him—hating him all over again.

'I didn't live with myself,' he said.

Flinging round to face him, she hated it too that he was

standing there looking and sounding so damn calm while she was falling apart! 'How is it that I got all the punishment while Marco remained your very best buddy?' she lanced at him. 'It did take two of us to cheat on you, after all!'

'I told you. He stopped being my friend.'

'So the story about him taking you home and putting you to bed the night I lost my baby was a lie, was it?'

'Now that was quick, considering the state you are in.' He dared to commend her with a brief smile. Then he lifted up a hand. 'Lexi—'

'Don't you *dare* say my name like you want to apologise to me,' she breathed shakily,

'We met up by accident in the bar I was in. I did not arrange to meet him there.' Grimly determined to get out the whole story, Franco ignored the way Lexi turned her back on him and continued doggedly on. 'When I saw him, I went to hit him but I was too drunk so I missed my target, fell on the floor, and basically passed out. Marco picked me up and took me back to my apartment. I don't remember anything after I crashed out on the bed.'

'Poor Claudia got her dearest wish to sleep with you and didn't care that you were comatose.' She swung round again. 'Is that the way you mean to tell it?'

'It was the only way it was going to happen, because I never felt a thing for her...not sexually anyway. Tell me,' he said then. 'Was I undressed?'

Mouth flattening tight, Lexi slumped back against the galley wall, frowned at her feet and gave no answer.

'I ask because I woke up the next morning with a thick head, still wearing my jeans,' Franco went on patiently.

'No T-shirt, though,' she whispered. All she'd seen in that cruel video was his top half, broad and bronzed against the sheet, with— 'Claudia was wearing a bra and pants.'

'Then use your head, *cara*, and think this through—'

'Stay back,' she threatened as he took a step her way.

'They planned it, Lexi,' he persisted, going still again. 'They wanted you out of my life. The video of me accepting the bet was just damn spitefulness on Claudia's side, but the other one was a coordinated plot between Marco and his sister to make you leave me. And he was ruthless about it. Who do you think it was who recorded the moment?'

*Marco.* Lexi tugged in a painful breath of air. 'Why, though?' She had to ask the question even though it hurt. 'He was your closest friend, and I thought he liked m-me.'

'I have come to realise that Marco only liked Marco,' he answered grimly. 'I've known him for over twenty years and turned a blind eye to most of his shortcomings. He was my friend and I—I cared about him. Until I believed he had slept with you.' Bleak cynicism cast a shadow across his face. 'What kind of friend betrays you by doing that?'

'What kind of lover betrays you by believing *I* could do that?'

'Fair point. No answer.' He held his hands out. 'I was young and arrogant and full of myself. I did not see why he should lie to me about something so important. He blamed you, and I was too willing to listen when he advised me to look at all the men you flirted with—the way you turned them on without seemingly knowing you were doing it.'

'I didn't do that!' Lexi gasped in hot denial, though she was already starting to blush. Back then she hadn't given much thought to what her happy go lucky flirtations were actually doing to the men she flirted with.

'Did you catch me coming onto other women?' Franco lanced at her.

'No.' Lexi dipped her head again, then felt forced to add, 'I used to drag you away when they came onto you.'

'Well, it was a very simple step for me to believe you could have taken your flirtation with Marco the next level.'

Had she flirted with Marco too? Yes, she'd flirted with Marco, Lexi accepted uncomfortably. He'd been the laid-back, sunny one of their crowd. Franco's best friend, whom she'd trusted and who'd always laughed and teased her about her practising her new found feminine wiles on him.

'He was in love you too, of course.'

Lexi blinked. 'I beg your pardon?'

'Marco,' he explained. 'When two friends fall out over a woman it usually means they are both in love with the same one... None of that is any kind of defence for the way I behaved during the months after we married. There *is* no defence,' he stated abruptly. 'But today, if you're willing, we can start again and try to do better this time.'

'Is that why we are here on the *Miranda*? To start again? Same venue, different odds?'

'The odds are up to you, Lexi.' He sounded so grim now, distant. 'I want us to work. The thing you need to ask yourself is do *you* want us to work? I need to check some things out on deck,' he added abruptly, and turned to disappear up the steps and out of sight.

Well, she thought once she was alone, *did* she want their marriage to work?

Of course she wanted it to work. She wasn't such a self-pitying klutz that she couldn't accept some of the responsibility for what had happened. After all, she hadn't exactly been the sweet, bewildered bride a man with Franco's proud personality could look at and find her melting his cold stance.

A long sigh broke free from her chest. So what was she going to do about it?

She noticed the uncapped bottle of water in her hand. She didn't really want it, so she turned to put it back in the fridge, wondering who it was who'd stocked the fridge for them, because most of the room was taken up with bottles of Franco's favourite beer.

Struck by a sudden idea, she took two bottles out and placed them on the galley top, then walked down the boat to push open a door at the far end that led into what was grandly described as a stateroom, though it was only big enough to take a double bed and set of drawers squeezed beside a cupboard.

Their two bags sat on the floor, and she'd bent to haul hers up on the bed with the intention of changing out of her sticky jeans when she saw them—the half dozen green frogs made of all kinds of shapes and materials, lined up in a row on the narrow shelf that ran the length of the bed. It was silly to feel weak tears sting her throat when she saw them sitting there, exactly where she'd left them, as if they'd been waiting patiently for her to return. It was even sillier to let a soft sob escape when she saw the grey rabbit sitting right in the middle of the row, as if he was making some kind of defiant statement to the frogs. Franco must have brought the rabbit with him and put it there. It had to have been the first thing he'd done when they'd arrived.

A sound made her turn, and she found him lounging in the narrow doorway, watching her through dark half-hooded eyes.

'You kept them,' she whispered.

'You expected me to throw them away?' His voice throbbed with dry challenge. 'They are yours, Lexi. They belong to you. They hold your dreams of a handsome prince and ideal love, which I obviously never lived up to.'

'Is that why you stuck the rabbit up there? To m-muscle in on my dreams?'

He looked at the rabbit, sitting there three times the size of its companions, and gave a crooked smile—because the rabbit *did* look as if he was muscling in on the frogs. 'No. He is there to represent me. My dreams. With a bit of luck on my side you will kiss the rabbit as you move along the row. Think of me, waiting for my turn.'

'I always thought of you when I kissed the frogs.'

'Your handsome prince?' He turned the crooked smile on her. 'I don't think so, *cara*. I let you down so badly I made a better villain in your fantasy world…' He straightened up and pulled in a deep breath. 'I came down to tell you I have to move the boat. There are rocks close to the surface. I cannot risk the *Miranda* swinging into one and damaging her hull. I've decided to use the sails. We will move much faster while there is a stiff breeze up. I need to find a safer place to anchor before it grows dark.'

'OK.' Lexi nodded her head, but he'd already turned away by then. 'I'll come and help. I…I just want to change out of these jeans and…' Her voice sounded so strained she was surprised when it trailed away to nothing. It took an effort to make it work again. She tried again. 'And you—you're still the only man I've been with…the only man I've wanted to be with… Can—can we talk about that instead of princes and villains and frogs?'

She could tell by the severe set of his shoulders that he would much rather escape right now. Franco had done a lot of opening up in the last hour, after spending too long holding it all in. Oh, they'd fought over many things during the last week, Lexi recognised—fought over other people's interference in their lives. But they hadn't touched base on what they were feeling—not really—not if she didn't count the time he'd told her he still loved her as they left the marina, and even that had become lost in the storm of shock she'd had straight afterwards.

'I do truly still love you too, Francesco,' she whispered shakily.

*'Madre di Dio!'* he swore, reeling back against the doorframe and spearing with her a burning glance. 'I have to move the damn boat, Lexi! And you throw this at me *now*?'

Her lips trembled as she parted them. 'I didn't throw it at you, I just—just told you s-so you would know.'

He closed his eyes. 'This is payback because I shocked you with such a declaration earlier.'

'Well, if you want to take it that way then go and play with your ropes and sails!' Lexi threw at him hotly. 'Because I am not repeating it!'

She spun away, and yelped when she was spun right back again. Two powerful arms hauled her up against his chest.

'That wasn't fair,' he growled.

'I know,' she admitted. 'I just got all h-heated up—'

A pair of eyes the colour of tiger's-eye quartz flamed down on her. He yanked her closer and fused their lips in a burning kiss. 'Now, *that's* heating you up, *amante mia*,' he taunted softly, then let go of her and disappeared through the door while Lexi stood, still burning.

The sails were up and they were running with the wind by the time Lexi came up on deck. Standing at the wheel, Franco watched her pause and raise her chin, letting the warmth of the wind blow her hair away from her face. She'd changed into the white bikini she'd been wearing by the pool for the last few days. A white sarong printed with flowers was draped around her hips, and she looked long and sleek and so much his kind of woman he smiled at himself for thinking it.

She was carrying two bottles of beer with the caps already removed.

'*Grazie,*' he said, when she handed him one of the bottles.

'Do you want me to do anything?'

'No, just come and stand here where I can see you.' He did not give her an option, just hooked an arm around her and drew her to stand in front of him.

As she settled against him Lexi saw he was in his element. With the sun on his face, the wind in the sails and the skimming hiss of water against the sides of the boat the only sound in a beautiful silence. This, she thought, was Franco's world.

'Do you have any idea where we are going?' she questioned curiously.

'*Si*, there is a pretty cove with a small beach and a restaurant within reach before the sun goes down.'

'Oh,' Lexi pouted. She didn't really want to leave the boat to eat in a restaurant. 'I didn't bring anything to wear suitable for eating out.'

He looked down at her, not fooled by her regretful tone in the slightest. 'I was not intending for us to eat there,' he drawled. 'I was merely describing the place we are heading for. I have other plans for dinner.'

'Zeta's pasta?' Lexi suggested.

Since she was glued to his front she knew exactly what he had planned for dinner. When he raised an eyebrow in that arrogant way he had she just laughed, kissed his chin, then turned around so she could lean back against him.

'Like the old times,' she murmured softly after a few minutes. 'I like this starting again.'

'No more questions? No more doubts?'

He spoke lightly, but Lexi knew there was a serious enquiry behind the question. They both knew they still had a lot of things to trawl out and work through, and they still had not talked about what had really happened when the *White Streak* crashed, but—

'I meant it before, when I said I wanted to talk about us— our feelings, not everyone else's feelings. They've messed up our lives enough as it is, but right now I just feel—scared.'

'Scared of what?'

She felt him grow tense behind her. 'That we're trying to recapture something here that shouldn't be recaptured. '

'You don't believe I still love you,' he declared after a second.

'I don't believe we've been back together long enough to know for sure *what* we are feeling,' she confided unhappily.

She watched his fingers tightening on the wheel. 'So I'm still on trial here?'

'I didn't say that—'

'You might as well have said that,' he countered.

'You should've told me what Marco said about me.'

'I know.' Lowering his head, he pressed a contrite kiss to the top of her head.

'I had a right to defend myself,' Lexi murmured.

'*Si,*' he agreed.

'And I had a right to have you trust me more than you did.'

'I know that too,' he accepted heavily. 'Marco knew all my weaknesses and he played on them. He was the only person I'd confided in that you were the one. I told him I was going to marry you, and do you know what he did?' Putting his bottle on the bulkhead freed him up to draw her even closer. 'He laughed like a drain. Then he asked if I would still want to marry you if I knew you had slept with him while I was away. I beat him up and threw him in the pool. When he climbed out he was still laughing. He wanted to know where the hell I got off, thinking I had exclusive rights on you. A bet was a bet.'

'But he must have known by then that you'd already won the bet!' Lexi protested. 'We hadn't exactly hidden the fact that we were lovers.'

'I wasn't thinking straight. I wanted to kill you. I wanted to kill him. Instead I turned myself into the ice man and brought the group together so I could claim my prize. I knew Claudia was recording the moment on her mobile, and I knew she would not be able to resist sending it to you. It was the salve for my wounded pride. The worst punishment I could come up with. I was saying, *Look how little you mean to me, Lexi Hamilton.*'

'It worked.' Lexi sniffed back a sob. 'I was devastated.'

'Then all the other stuff happened,' Franco continued bleakly. 'Your mother and Philippe Reynard were killed. I had distanced myself from you by then but you looked so lost I couldn't get back in there quick enough to give you support.'

'Then I discovered I was pregnant.'

'And I behaved like a spoilt, heartless brat. I loved you, but it scared me to love you. I couldn't marry you fast enough, but

I made you feel like you had ruined my life. When you left me I beat myself up for driving you away, but my bruised pride would not let me go chasing after you. When I did eventually pluck up the nerve to come and see you I got to see Dayton instead.'

'Let's not go there,' Lexi said quickly. 'I've spoken to him. He knows I know what he did, and he knows our friendship is over for good.'

'As Claudia knows,' Franco concluded. 'As Marco knew when we argued before the race.' He took in a deep breath, then told her what had happened. 'I knew he was going to do something crazy when he said goodbye to me,' he said thickly. 'I never meant to drive him to the point of—'

'It wasn't your fault.' Lexi turned to put her arms around him and looked at him anxiously. 'You have got to stop thinking that it was. You spoke so beautifully about him today, Franco,' she reminded him softly. 'Remember Marco as that person—the one you loved as a brother.'

They arrived at their destination then, and the boat demanded their attention. Perhaps it was a good thing, because it gave them time to detach themselves from the ugliness of the past—to throw it all away for good. They worked well together, in unison, like they'd used to do—as Franco had taught her all those years ago. Then they cooked Zeta's pasta and took it up on deck to eat beneath the stars, drinking beer out of the bottles like they'd used to.

It was pretty much an exact replay of that perfect summer, Lexi thought as she sat cross-legged on the deck beside Franco's outstretched strong golden legs and watched the restaurant lights beyond the tiny cove shine softly in the distance.

Yet there was still one small question that begged an answer. 'What made you decide that Marco had been lying about me?' she murmured softly.

He didn't say anything for such a long time Lexi felt all

the tension start to creep back. Then he heaved in a deep breath and reached for her, lifting her up to bring her down so she straddled his warm thighs. His eyes were dark in the soft light from the single lantern they'd lit. He looked sombre and thoughtful as he gently combed a lock of her hair away from her cheek.

'Let me tell, instead, what loving you meant to me,' he murmured deeply. 'Loving you, *anima mia*, meant losing the ability to focus for long on anything without thinking about you. It meant checking the phone a hundred times a day in case you'd called. It meant walking into a room and searching it in case you might be there, and waking in the middle of the night with your name on my lips and your perfume in my nose and the taste—*Dio*,' he husked, 'the taste of you on my tongue. It meant I was lonely in a crowd of people. It was the joke I laughed at while I was crying inside, and the nagging ache that constantly dogged me low down in my gut, always there, driving me insane—yet the hell of it was I never wanted it to go away.'

Close to tears, Lexi pressed her fingers against his lips. 'Please don't say any more,' she whispered. 'You're breaking my heart.'

'My heart was broken,' he said, reaching up to remove her fingers, kissing them, then keeping hold of them. 'Don't cry. When you cry it tears me apart. Loving you was wishing, and hating myself for wishing, and wanting you so badly. I used to conjure up the image Marco had put in my head of you with him, but the image always faded to show me just you. *This* Lexi,' he described softly. 'The one with the toffee-gold hair and the ocean-green eyes—loving *me*. Loving me, Lexi. And you never stopped, did you? After everything I did to murder your feelings for me, you could not stop loving me either. I saw it from the moment I looked into your beautiful face.'

'Are you saying that you *didn't* bring me back to Italy because you realised that Marco had been lying to you?'

Reaching up, he ran the tip of a finger along the trembling line of her mouth. 'I did tell you several times that I'd already been planning to see you before the crash happened,' he reminded her. 'I just wanted you back. Your divorce papers gave me one hell of a jolt. They made me realise it was time to stop fighting myself, put the thing with Marco behind me and fight to get you back. Then, as I flew through the air that day and wondered if I was going to survive, it came to me in a blinding flash that Marco had lied to me. He had implied as much before the race, but...'

'It doesn't matter,' Lexi put in quickly. She did not want to think of him flying through the air, believing he was going to die. 'I love you, Franco,' she murmured urgently. 'In every single way you just described about me, but I don't want—'

Whatever it was Lexi did not want became lost when Franco captured her mouth in a hungry, hot, passionate kiss. Before she knew it she'd lost her bikini top and they were lying flat on the deck, making love in the velvet darkness—the way they'd used to do.

Later they went to the stateroom, holding hands all the way even though it made moving through the narrow doorways almost impossible.

'You forgot to kiss the frogs,' Franco said as they came together beneath the sheets.

'To hell with the frogs,' Lexi responded irreverently. 'It's you I want to kiss.'

\* \* \* \* \*

# CLASSIC

**COMING NEXT MONTH from Harlequin Presents® EXTRA**
AVAILABLE APRIL 10, 2012

### #193 SAVAS'S WILDCAT
*Return of the Rebels*
**Anne McAllister**

### #194 THE DEVIL AND MISS JONES
*Return of the Rebels*
**Kate Walker**

### #195 THE EX WHO HIRED HER
*The Ex Files*
**Kate Hardy**

### #196 THE EX FACTOR
*The Ex Files*
**Anne Oliver**

**COMING NEXT MONTH from Harlequin Presents®**
AVAILABLE APRIL 24, 2012

### #3059 RETURN OF THE MORALIS WIFE
**Jacqueline Baird**

### #3060 THE PRICE OF ROYAL DUTY
*The Santina Crown*
**Penny Jordan**

### #3061 A DEAL AT THE ALTAR
*Marriage by Command*
**Lynne Graham**

### #3062 A NIGHT OF LIVING DANGEROUSLY
**Jennie Lucas**

### #3063 A WILD SURRENDER
**Anne Mather**

### #3064 GIRL BEHIND THE SCANDALOUS REPUTATION
*Scandal in the Spotlight*
**Michelle Conder**

HPCNM0412

# REQUEST YOUR
# FREE BOOKS!

## 2 FREE NOVELS PLUS
## 2 FREE GIFTS!

PASSION
GUARANTEED
SEDUCTION

**YES!** Please send me 2 FREE Harlequin Presents® novels and my 2 FREE gifts (gifts are worth about $10). After receiving them, if I don't wish to receive any more books, I can return the shipping statement marked "cancel." If I don't cancel, I will receive 6 brand-new novels every month and be billed just $4.30 per book in the U.S. or $4.99 per book in Canada. That's a saving of at least 14% off the cover price! It's quite a bargain! Shipping and handling is just 50¢ per book in the U.S. and 75¢ per book in Canada.* I understand that accepting the 2 free books and gifts places me under no obligation to buy anything. I can always return a shipment and cancel at any time. Even if I never buy another book, the two free books and gifts are mine to keep forever.

106/306 HDN FERQ

| Name | (PLEASE PRINT) | |
|---|---|---|
| Address | | Apt. # |
| City | State/Prov. | Zip/Postal Code |

Signature (if under 18, a parent or guardian must sign)

Mail to the **Reader Service:**
**IN U.S.A.:** P.O. Box 1867, Buffalo, NY 14240-1867
**IN CANADA:** P.O. Box 609, Fort Erie, Ontario L2A 5X3

Not valid for current subscribers to Harlequin Presents books.

**Are you a current subscriber to Harlequin Presents books
and want to receive the larger-print edition?
Call 1-800-873-8635 or visit www.ReaderService.com.**

\* Terms and prices subject to change without notice. Prices do not include applicable taxes. Sales tax applicable in N.Y. Canadian residents will be charged applicable taxes. Offer not valid in Quebec. This offer is limited to one order per household. All orders subject to credit approval. Credit or debit balances in a customer's account(s) may be offset by any other outstanding balance owed by or to the customer. Please allow 4 to 6 weeks for delivery. Offer available while quantities last.

**Your Privacy**—The Reader Service is committed to protecting your privacy. Our Privacy Policy is available online at www.ReaderService.com or upon request from the Reader Service.

We make a portion of our mailing list available to reputable third parties that offer products we believe may interest you. If you prefer that we not exchange your name with third parties, or if you wish to clarify or modify your communication preferences, please visit us at www.ReaderService.com/consumerschoice or write to us at Reader Service Preference Service, P.O. Box 9062, Buffalo, NY 14269. Include your complete name and address.

**Harlequin** *Romance*

*Award-winning author*

# DONNA ALWARD

*brings you two rough-and-tough
cowboys with hearts of gold.*

CADENCE CREEK
COWBOYS

## They're the Rough Diamonds of the West

From the moment Sam Diamond turned up late to her
charity's meeting, placating everyone with a tip of his Stetson
and a lazy smile, Angela Beck knew he was trouble.

Angela is the most stubborn, beautiful woman Sam's ever met
and he'd love to still her sharp tongue with a kiss, but first
he has to get close enough to uncover the complex woman
beneath. And that's something only a real cowboy can do....

## THE LAST REAL COWBOY

*Available in May.*

And look for Tyson Diamond's story,

## THE REBEL RANCHER,

*coming this June!*

HR17807

**Stop The Press!** *Crown Prince in Shock Marriage*

When Crown Prince Alessandro of Santina
proposes to paparazzi favorite Allegra Jackson
it promises to be *the* social event of the decade!

Discover all 8 stories in the scandalous
new miniseries THE SANTINA CROWN
from Harlequin Presents®!

\*\*\*

*Enjoy this sneak peek from Penny Jordan's*
*THE PRICE OF ROYAL DUTY,*
*book 1 in* THE SANTINA CROWN *miniseries.*

"DON'T YOU THINK you're being a tad dramatic?" he
asked her in a wry voice.

"I'm not being dramatic," she defended herself. "Surely
I should have some rights as a person, a human being, some
say in my own fate, instead of having my future decided
for me by my father. To endure marriage to a man who has
simply agreed to marry me because he wants an heir, and to
whom my father has virtually auctioned me off in exchange
for a royal alliance."

"I should have thought such a marriage would suit you,
Sophia. After all, it's well documented that your own cho-
sen lifestyle involves something very similar, when it comes
to bed hopping."

A body blow indeed, and one that drove the blood from
Sophia's face and doubled the pain in her heart. It shouldn't
matter what Ash thought of her. That was not part of her
plan. But still his denunciation of her hurt, and it wasn't one

EXP0412

she could defend herself against. Not without telling him far more than she wanted him to know.

"Then you thought wrong" was all she could permit herself to say. "That is not the kind of marriage I want. I can't bear the thought of this marriage." Her panic and fear were there in her voice; even she could hear it herself, so how much more obvious must it be to Ash?

She must try to stay calm. Not even to Ash could she truly explain the distaste, the loathing, the fear she had of being forced by law to give herself in a marriage bed in the most intimate way possible when... No, that was one secret that she must keep no matter what, just as she had already kept it for so long. "Please, Ash, I'm begging you for your help."

*Will Ash discover Sophia's secret?*
*Find out in THE PRICE OF ROYAL DUTY*
*by*
USA TODAY *bestselling author*
**Penny Jordan**

*Book 1 of* THE SANTINA CROWN *miniseries*
*available May 2012 from Harlequin Presents®!*